D0340613

FOR BLACK GIRLS LIKE ME

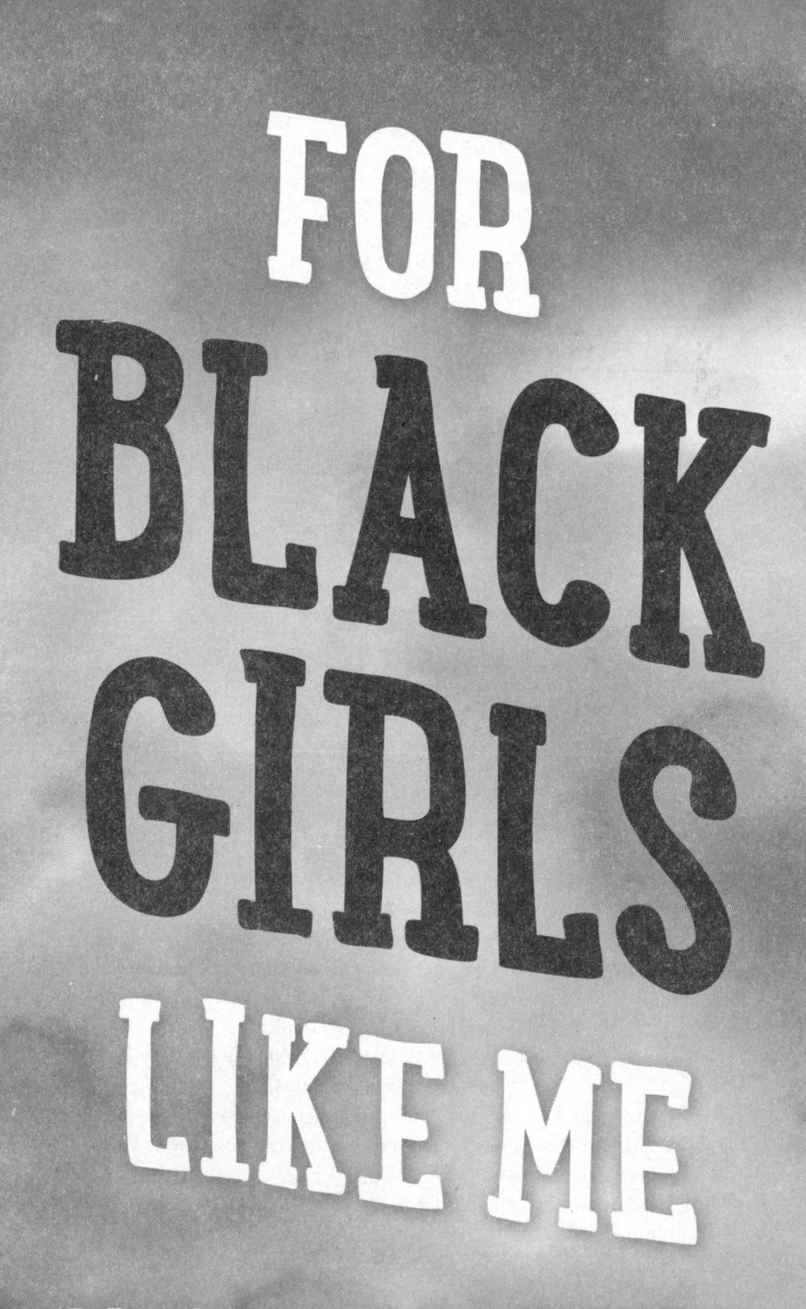
FOR
BLACK
GIRLS
LIKE ME
Mariama J. Lockington
Farrar Straus Giroux • New York

Farrar Straus Giroux Books for Young Readers
An imprint of Macmillan Publishing Group, LLC
120 Broadway, New York, NY 10271

Printed in the United States of America by
LSC Communications, Harrisonburg, Virginia
Designed by Aimee Fleck
First edition, 2019

1 3 5 7 9 10 8 6 4 2

mackids.com

Library of Congress Cataloging-in-Publication Data

Names: Lockington, Mariama, author.
Title: For black girls like me / Mariama J. Lockington.
Description: First edition. | New York : Farrar Straus Giroux, 2019. | Summary: Eleven-year-old Makeda dreams of meeting her African American mother, while coping with serious problems in her white adopted family, a cross-country move, and being homeschooled.
Identifiers: LCCN 2018035461 | ISBN 9780374308049 (hardcover) | ISBN (ebook) 9780374308063
Subjects: | CYAC: Identity—Fiction. | African Americans—Fiction. | Interracial adoption—Fiction. | Family problems—Fiction. | Home schooling—Fiction. | Moving, Household—Fiction.
Classification: LCC PZ7.1.L6235 For 2019 | DDC [Fic]—dc23
LC record available at https://lccn.loc.gov/2018035461

For my siblings—E, D & I

Part I: SPRING

Tumbleweeds . . . 3
In Broken Arrow Oklahoma . . . 5
Family Names . . . 7
Time Passes on the Road . . . 9
Somewhere in Texas . . . 11
I Have a Secret . . . 13
She . . . 16
Classical Music . . . 17
As We Drive Through the Red Desert . . . 19
Are We There Yet?! . . . 23
My New Room . . . 26
First Impressions . . . 28
Boxes . . . 30
How It All Began . . . 32
El Rio Charter Academy . . . 34
20 Questions . . . 36
After School . . . 39
Little House on the Prairie . . . 42
6th Grade War Games . . . 44
Improvising . . . 53
Imagining Mama as a Girl . . . 57
After Breakfast . . . 59
Dictionary . . . 62
Back to School . . . 64
Letters from Lena . . . 65
In the Locker Room . . . 74

Blackmail 77
I Do Have a Crush 79
There Are Terrible Songs in Me 82
I Start to Question 84
Saturday April 16th 87
The Friday Mixer 89
Questions I Have for Black Girls Like Me 91
Maps 92
The Short Drive Home 95
Questions for HER 98
Betrayed 99
Sisters 102
The Georgia Belles 105
Our Bodies Ourselves 107
Top Secret 111
Chicks 115
New Routines 116

Questions I Have for Black Girls Like Me
posted April 25th 119

Homeschool Group 121
We Spend the Next Two Days Cleaning 123
Tangled 127
Huckleberry Finn 135
Hot Springs 139
Moonlight Sonata 144
Insomnia (noun) 146

Part II: SUMMER

June in the Desert 153
Sweet Tomato 155
My Bike 158
Happy Birthday America 161
Girl Scouts 167

Questions I Have for Black Girls Like Me
posted July 5th 171

In This House We Believe 173
Melody Icey 177
Never Forget 182
The Boy Book 184
Fireball 188
Upside Down 190

Questions I Have for Black Girls Like Me
posted July 12th 194

Fire 196
"DO YOU LOVE IT? I LOVE IT! I GOT IT AT ROSS!" 197

Questions I Have for Black Girls Like Me
posted July 17th 200

Flying 201
Boulder 203
After 206
The River 209
Needles & Yarn 211
No More Sweatpants and Frumpy Shirts 214
Safe 217
Practice Makes Perfect 221
Exploring 224
A Girlhood Is a Terrible-Wonderful Time 226
Fun Fun Fun 229
Independent Women 231
Even the Aspen Trees 233
Suicide (noun) 235
Aunt Sarah 237
Reunion 239
Psychiatric Evaluation (noun) 242
Blessings 245
It's a Hard-Knock Life 247
Small 252

Part III: FALL

Labor Day Weekend 257
Mother (noun) 260
A Gloomy Sunday 262
Bad Jokes 266
Brightree Clinic and Retreat 268
Hereditary (adjective) 274
Showing 276
Inheritance 278
Reset 282
I Have a Secret Wish 283
New Faces 285
Lists 288
Telling. 290
Imagining Lady Day's Return 293
Chances 295
State Capitol 297

Questions I Have for Black Girls Like Me
posted October 17th 300

Questions I Have for Black Girls Like Me
posted October 19th 302

Kin (noun) 305
Family Fridays 307

Mama Is in the Earth 310
Lessons 312
Flung 315
What I Know 317

"I'm me. Me." Each time she said the word *me* there was a gathering in her like power, like joy, like fear . . . "Me," she murmured. And then, sinking deeper into her quilts, "I want . . . I want to be . . . wonderful. Oh, Jesus, make me wonderful."

—Toni Morrison, *Sula*

Kindred spirits are not so scarce as I used to think. It's splendid to find out there are so many of them in the world.

—L. M. Montgomery, *Anne of Green Gables*

Part I: SPRING

Tumbleweeds

I am a girl but most days I feel like a question mark. People throw their looks at me. Then back at my mama sister and papa. Who are all as white as oleander. Then they look back at me. Black as a midnight orchard. And I see their puzzled faces trying to understand where I fit. People ask me where I'm from but I know they really mean

Who do you belong to?

Right now I am on the road. Somewhere just outside of St. Louis. It's March. Our second day of driving cross-country from Baltimore to our new house in Albuquerque. I sit in the middle seat of the minivan with the windows cracked. My ashy legs spotted with sunshine. My older sister Eve in the seat behind me. Her glossy brown hair blowing in the breeze. Mama is up front with one hand on the wheel. Her violin in the passenger seat. The neck tipped down like a bottle being emptied into the sink. All of us heading west. A copper sun warming the sky. All of us singing along with the radio at the top of our lungs.

And Mama has a smile on her face this morning. Her freckled cheeks flushed red as a juneberry as she sings and rolls the front windows down so that the whole van becomes a whistle. The wind whips in and out of our throats our eyes our hair and I forget my ashy knees. I forget to miss my best friend Lena who I've left behind. The only other girl I know who is like me. An adopted mismatched girl. I forget to be angry at Papa for missing another family adventure. For having to fly ahead of us to start his new job with the symphony. I forget to worry about Mama and Papa always fighting these days. Mama staring wildly through windows. Hardly playing her violin at all.

For hours we drive and sing the sun into its highest point in the sky. *This is where I am from!* I whisper-yell between verses. And for a moment I hope we might stay like this forever. Me Mama and Eve. A tangled smear of color barreling past ghost towns and highway markers. Three tumbleweeds just blowing in the wind.

In Broken Arrow Oklahoma

Mama and Eve grab snacks from the rest stop mini-mart while I lounge in the driver's seat pretending I am grown. *Beep beep!* I air honk the horn. "Look out world. I'm coming. Are you ready?" But the rumble in my stomach is the only answer I get. It's past lunchtime.

The road is the only place we are allowed junk food. Normally it's organic meat. Limp veggies. Strange grains like barley millet and quinoa. Snacks of apple slices and carrot sticks. Beet and sweet potato chips. And forget about Halloween candy or birthday cakes. "When you're eighteen" Mama says "you can eat all the candy and processed sugar you want since you'll be paying your own dentist bills!"

But being on the road changes the rules. There's nothing but gas station food Taco Bells and greasy diners off I-40 West. Mama and Eve walk back to the van now with armfuls of the healthiest junk food they can find. Pretzels honey-roasted peanuts dark chocolate bars and more. I climb into the middle seat and Eve jumps in the back and tears open a bag of baked Lay's.

"Lemme have a chip!" I say.

Eve plunges her hand into the bag and pulls out a huge handful which she then crushes into her mouth.

"You're disgusting."

"Gim-mme-a-kiss!" She leans forward. An avalanche of chip pieces spewing from her mouth.

I crack a smile and snatch the bag from her.

Mama revs the engine and yells: "Seatbelts on!" And then to me: "Are you sure you don't need to pee?"

"Nope. No thanks! Rest stop bathrooms are gross."

"Ok. Your choice. But I'm not stopping again until dinner."

I look at the time on the dashboard. It's only 2pm. Dinner won't be until around 7 but the thought of going out into another bathroom and facing the eyes of confused clerks and customers as they try to figure out where I came from makes my stomach knot. Before I can change my mind Mama is speeding out onto the road. I cross my legs and whip my head around. I watch the gas pumps greasy truck drivers and low buildings disappear into a cloud of dirt.

Family Names

Daniel Anna

Eve

Makeda

One of these is not like the rest.

Eve is fourteen. Three years older than me and the biological child of our parents. Their "miracle baby" since Mama was told she'd never be able to have kids. Eve has the same thick brown hair and pale complexion as Mama and Papa and sometimes when you look at pictures of Mama from childhood you'd swear you were looking right at Eve.

Eve used to be a lot more fun but these days all she seems to care about are her pores texting or complaining about her mysterious "cramps" at the most inconvenient times. Even now she hogs the whole back seat with her stacks of *Seventeen* magazines (which I am not allowed to read yet) and ignores me as I try to get her to play the license plate game.

I am eleven. All elbow and chubby cheek with a baby smile and fuzzy rows of tight dreadlocks crowning my head. Where my face is round the rest of my body is what the white boys at my old school used to say is "Africa skinny" with lean arms. Thin legs and a little potbelly that peeks out from under my tops and elastic-waisted skirts.

"Those boys just don't realize how elegant you are!" Mama likes to tell me on days I come home with war in my eyes. "Always remember you're my little African princess."

But I'm not African. I'm African American. It always bothers me when she says this. I was born in Atlanta Georgia then adopted after six months. I flew with a social worker to Baltimore to meet my family and it was Mama who gave me my name. *Makeda June Kirkland.*

June because that's what my birth mother called me. Kirkland because that's Papa's last name. And Makeda. An Ethiopian name meaning "Queen of Sheba" all because Mama read an article about famine in Ethiopia and decided to name me after a girl listed among the dead.

"We got you almost one year after I read that story! Our own beautiful black baby. Soft as a peach." Mama likes to tell. "And I just knew I had to name you after that poor girl. I knew she would live on in you. My Makeda."

I like Keda for short. I am not a dead girl.

Time Passes on the Road

But you wouldn't know it except for the sun sliding its way down the sky like an egg yolk. Three hours later we are somewhere in the middle of nowhere. Nothing but prairie livestock and small towns for miles and miles on end. Eve naps and snores loudly while I sit twisting a hair tie around my thumb watching all the color drain from it. In the front seat Mama listens to recordings of her own from the old days. Mama is a solo violinist. She played with her first symphony at the age of eight. Had visited over twenty countries by the time she was my age and had played in Carnegie Hall in New York City twice before either Eve or I came along in her early twenties.

"I *was* a prodigy." She likes to remind us. "But then I decided to start a family. And that changes everything for a woman."

She always says that last part. About being a woman. So that it prickles my ears. Her voice turning small and grainy as if she's been swallowing rocks. And even though she has hardly played her violin for the last year (since she got let go from her teaching job at a private school) it sits now in the passenger side taking up a whole seat Eve and I would kill for. We know better than to ask her to move it or comment on how little she's practiced. We also know better than to bother her when she starts reminiscing about past concerts and recordings. Sibelius Concerto in D Minor booms now from the speakers and Mama's right hand escapes the wheel to saw through the air in bow-like movements along with the track. Her long braid hangs over her right shoulder like an old friend and for a moment I catch her closing her eyes lost in some enormous swell of sound. Before I can say anything the car passing us on the left honks and Mama swerves back into her lane.

"Jerk!" She flips the car off as it speeds past. Tears bursting from her eyes and disappearing into the canyon of her lap. She switches off her recording and fiddles with the radio for a moment but we are in a dead zone and only a few static Christian radio stations come through. "Sing me something Makeda." She says after a while. "Or else I'm going to fall asleep up here."

And something heavy in her voice warns me not to say no. So I start to hum some made-up tune until the radio kicks back in and Mama's face dries into a hard-smooth shine.

Somewhere in Texas

We stop for dinner. Mama lets us order hamburgers even though she's pretty sure we're putting ourselves at risk for mad cow disease. She orders a sad-looking salad while Eve and I slather our plates in so much ketchup our table looks like a mini crime scene. We eat like wolves. No napkins no forks. We stuff as many fries as we can fit into our mouths. Burger grease drips down our arms.

"Honestly girls." Mama interrupts. "Slow down! Your food's not going anywhere." But we are too hungry to care. Mama picks and picks at her salad and then steps outside to give Papa a call. We watch through the glass windows as she dials and sets her lips in a firm line.

"Blah blah blah. You son of a b— this drive is killing me. I can't believe you left me to do it alone!" Eve starts to interpret their conversation pretending that her fork is Mama and the spoon is Papa. We can't hear what Mama is actually saying but she's been complaining to Papa since he left last week.

"Honey." Eve continues now in Papa's soft voice. "You're more than halfway here! I promise it's going to be worth it when you see the house. It's beautiful. With a huge yard. I have everything set up. Blah blah blah."

And then again in Mama's voice. "You better or I'm going to turn this van around and head right back! What about my career huh? What good does this move do for me?"

"Stop it!" I giggle even though I feel like throwing up. "You don't know what they're talking about."

Eve snorts and drops the spoon and fork back on the table. "Don't be so stupid Keda. You know it's some version of that."

I look outside. Mama is tugging at her braid. Twisting it around her wrist over and over again. The thin line of her mouth has transformed into a pink gash flashing teeth and spit as she yell-cries into her phone. Above her head moths swarm a piss-colored fluorescent light creating the illusion of a rain cloud directly over her. Eve rolls her eyes and gets up to use the restroom. I stick my hand into my water glass and stir the ice until they both return. Then I shove my numb fingers into my mouth and bite down as hard as I can.

I Have a Secret

Shadows in my room at night
Two women swaying
In the dark-light
At first I am afraid
They are as tall as trees
They surround my bed
And lean over me
Their breath sweet and sticky
Scent of sap and summer
The wind of their movement
Fluttering the sheets
My eyelashes
At first all I can make out
Is a low hum
A river-thick rush of sound
But here in the Texas night
Tucked away in a Motel 6
Mama and Eve snoring softly

For the first time

Since they started visiting a month ago

I understand they are singing *to* me

Outside the highway hurries by

The bare moon blinking

Through the thin curtains

And like always

I am still awake

Scared and full of worry

"You followed me?"

I whisper

As they approach

We go where you go

Baby girl baby girl

They sing

And I want to tell them

I am not

A baby anymore

Everything is changing

But they sing

So I close my eyes

We go where you go

Baby girl baby girl

My breath slows

And I fall

Into a dream

About her

She

Is a woman with no face and no name

My birth mother

Everything I know about her

Is in my adoption file

I lived in her womb for nine months

She gave birth to me on December 8th

She was a freshman in college when she had me

She decided not to keep me

She picked my family as her first choice

She could not keep me

She did not *want* to keep me?

I love her

Some days I hate her

I dream and dream of her everywhere I go

Classical Music

Is a big deal in our family. In fact *it's your legacy!* Papa likes to remind us when Eve and I start to whine about practicing piano for one hour each day. I HATE the piano but the next morning as we wash our faces and pack the van back up for our final day of driving I am a little lighter knowing our baby grand is stuffed deep into the moving truck with all of our other belongings. No practicing on the road!

Papa is strict about what goes in and out of our ears. He's a cellist. Now the principal cellist of the New Mexico Symphony and both he and Mama have been playing classical music since they were little kids. In our house we listen to old dead guy composers like Chopin Bach Brahms Vivaldi Tchaikovsky Schumann Mendelssohn Beethoven and more. But when Papa is not around we can convince Mama to let us listen to almost anything we want. I like Beyoncé and Katy Perry but I also really love jazz and the blues. And besides this is the only black music I'm allowed to listen to. "No rap! No hip-hop! No R and B!" Papa likes to lecture us. "It's just a bunch of noise and gibberish!" It makes my tongue go numb when he says this. Do I sound like gibberish when I sing?

“Can we listen to ‘A-Tisket A-Tasket’?” I ask as Mama turns onto the highway.

“Sure. That sounds nice.”

And as the van revs up to full speed Ella Fitzgerald’s voice climbs with it. And I don’t care if it is old or sounds scratchy and fuzzy playing on the speakers. I love Ella and Billie Holiday and oh I just can’t get enough of Nina Simone. These women sing and I feel like they are talking to me. Like we are speaking the same language. Like they know what it is to feel loved and lonely all at the same time.

As We Drive Through the Red Desert

I miss the green of Baltimore. I miss my best friend Lena. I miss playing under the willow tree in her backyard dreaming of college and boys. Lena and I met in the 2nd grade in a playgroup for adopted kids. All the other kids were Asian or white but Lena was black like me. Lena was adopted from Haiti when she was a baby. Her parents are white white white. Dutch white. When we met I didn't have to explain to her who my "real parents" were or why I "talked so proper" or prove to her that Eve was really my sister. She just knew. And even though we went to different schools we became fast friends. In the summer we'd float side by side in the pool. Two brown islands holding hands in the water. The dogwoods looming over us like green giants. Cicadas hissing all through the leaves.

The day we said goodbye we left the shelter of the willow and walked down to the creek at the bottom of her parents' property.

"Here." Lena said handing over a bright purple composition notebook. "Write me in here and then send it to me after a month or so. Then I'll write you back."

"Have you heard of an email?" I laughed.

"Yeah yeah but this way it's secret. Our parents won't read it. We can email too. And when our parents finally let us get cell phones we can text."

I hugged her hard. "We should make some sort of promise. To be friends no matter what." I said.

"Ok. I like that."

I found two small black stones at the edge of the water. "Here. Let's promise on these."

We stood holding the stones and each other's hands. We didn't talk. We squeezed our eyes shut and then whispered "*FOR-EVER*." Then we threw the rocks into the creek.

I don't remember saying goodbye. I only remember that my whole body ached. That the climb back up to her house was much too short. And then I was leaving her for good.

Now in the van I open the purple notebook and steady it on my knees.

Thursday March 10th

L

We just crossed the state line into New Mexico. We're gonna be at our new house soon!

Wish you could see how red it is here. Not one willow tree in sight. Eve doesn't even care about the scenery changing. She sleeps through it all. ***EYE ROLL*** But I'm awake.

Did you know that the desert gets REALLY cold? Like 35 degrees at night and in the morning. But it heats up in the middle of the day with the sun. I thought the desert was supposed to be hot all the time? Just another thing my parents forgot to mention. I start at my new school on Monday and I'm nervous. It's going to be hard starting in the middle of the year. What if nobody wants to talk to me?

At least I have you.

Anyway. I'll let you know if there are any cute boys. Did you know the mountains in Albuquerque are called the "Sandias" because they turn pink like watermelons at sunset? Oh! And that a lot of the houses here are single-story and made of a mud called "adobe"? Everything here is the color of fire and burnt things.

My skin feels so dry. I'll email you some pictures soon.

XO

K

Are We There Yet?!

"We're here." Mama says pulling onto a long dirt road a few hours later.

Maryland Pennsylvania West Virginia Ohio Indiana Illinois Missouri Oklahoma Texas and New Mexico. Ten states and three days later we finally arrive in Albuquerque. It's midafternoon and the sun has turned the valley into a simmering bowl of dry air.

"Thank you sweet baby Jesus!" I yell. Stretching my cramped legs.

"Keda. You know we don't believe in Jesus. Why do you always say that? We're humanists." Mama says. Snapping her head around to glare at me.

"Geez. It's just an expression."

"Where are we?" Eve sits up now and rubs the sleep out of her eyes.

"At our new house." I almost yell.

"It looks like the middle of nowhere to me." Eve grunts.

"It's on some land." Mama replies.

"How much land?" I ask. "Bigger than our yard in Baltimore?"

"At least five times bigger. One acre."

"Oh great!" Eve continues. "So we live in the country now. Like a bunch of smelly organic hippies."

"We kinda are hippies." I say. "I mean. At least the way we eat."

"Girls. We are not hippies. We are environmentally conscious women. We just care about what we put in our bodies. What we leave on this earth. I for one am going to make the best of this land. It means I can finally start a little farm."

"Sounds like some hippie BS to me." Eve mutters as we pull up to a set of metal gates held together by a big chain.

"Makeda jump out and get the gate!" Mama yells ignoring Eve's tone.

I unhook the big chain from one corner of the gate and jump onto it as it swings open. Mama continues in and I run up the driveway behind the van to our new house. The driveway is long and lined with crab apple trees. The house at the end is made of adobe the color of pennies at the bottom of a jar. It's long and L-shaped with a big sunroom peeking off the back-left side. And Papa is here. He comes out of the front door grinning with his crooked front teeth and gray hair that looks like a mop. I run right into his arms.

"There's my little chocolate scoop!" He teases. "And my big vanilla scoop!" He says to Eve who sticks out her tongue as she climbs out of the back seat and nuzzles into his embrace anyway. "My two girls. Sweet like the perfect bowl of ice cream. Welcome home!"

And Mama doesn't join us. She walks past us. Into the house. As if she knows where she's going. *How rude!* I think. But then I run inside after her to claim my room.

My New Room

Is painted a happy-face yellow. The polished wood floors are lined with a thin coat of dust and there is one big window looking out eastward onto the front yard. My bed is already set up but everything else is in boxes. My new room sits at the very end of a long hallway. My new room is twice as big as the room Eve and I shared in Baltimore. It even has a double closet lined with mirrors. I sit on my bed and look at my reflection. I feel so small. I hear Eve unpacking her things. Playing music softly from her phone. Her room is right across from mine and the exact same size except it faces the backyard.

"Eve!" I yell.

"What?" She says peeking out from her door.

"Want to have a sleepover in my room tonight?"

"Not really."

"Please?"

"Keda. We just got here ok? We need to get used to being in our own rooms. I'm too old for sleepovers."

"Fine." But my face is hot. I don't get what's changed. In Baltimore we used to wait until Mama tucked us in and then I would climb into Eve's bed and we'd whisper about our days. And when it would thunderstorm Eve would let me bury my face in her hair.

"Don't be scared." She'd say. "It's just the sky putting on a show for us!" And she'd let me stay until the storm passed.

But then Eve started 9th grade. She got a cell phone and instead of gossiping with me she stays up under her covers chatting with her friends or watching musical theater videos. She never looks up from that stupid thing!

Who needs her anyway? I get up from my bed and close my door. I stand in the middle of MY NEW ROOM. I hear Papa begin to practice in the sunroom. The low notes of his cello vibrating through the walls of the house like the dull throb of a stubbed toe. I open my window and smell bonfire smoke from a nearby property. And then I see it. The mountains are covered in the messy light of the setting sun. And they really are a deep watermelon pink.

First Impressions

Tall throbbing mountains
Dust in the eye
Gaping cliffs
Everywhere I look
A hurt
Even the dusk
A scab
The horizon hard
Leering
That first night
I fight sleep
Curl in and out
Of thicket dreams
Wake to more distance
More red red rock-ache
"How do soft things
Grow here?"
I whisper
The two women

Appear even clearer

In my new room

You will see

You will see

Baby girl baby girl

The Georgia Belles

Are here and we go

Where you go

But I am panicked

"How will **she** ever

Find me now?"

You will see

Baby girl baby girl

A mother never forgets

Boxes

The next day Papa leaves for a weekend of concerts in Santa Fe so Mama Eve and I spend all day unpacking boxes and taking breaks to slide around on the wood floors in nothing but our socks and underwear. When we get too tired we sit on the screened-in porch listening to the wild dogs. The strange Albuquerque desert notes. The house begins to fill with empty boxes. Some collapsed. Some so large I climb in and close the tops over my head. Some with holes worn through the sides from the jam-packed moving truck that brought all our things from Baltimore.

I start collecting all of the empties. The big ones. Even some of the ones with holes. Holes make good windows for spying. I stack the boxes in the backyard binding them together with duct tape to make long tunnels. Different mismatched rooms.

Mama is crabby all weekend. And even though she's always telling us to be creative she yells: "You have a perfectly good room of your own. Put those boxes in the recycling!"

Eve won't even look inside of my box fort but I keep at it. I bring blankets and my songbook and pens. I graffiti the cardboard walls with my favorite words: *home violet sky.* And when it gets dark out I turn on my flashlight and read until Mama screams to get in the house for bed.

"You're not a hobo you know." Eve foams at the mouth as we brush our teeth for bed. "You belong inside."

Inside. That's another one of my favorite words. I can't explain how the box fort makes me feel but it is something like what I imagine the word *inside* feels like. And when the rainstorm comes on Sunday afternoon along with the return of Papa. I sit on the back porch and watch my boxes collapse. No. Melt into the dirt grass. And I do not cry. Instead I hum. Then I sing *inside inside gone gone gone.*

How It All Began

That night before bed I crawl next to Papa on the futon couch. "Tell me about my special day please?" We are in the sunroom and Papa takes off his reading glasses and sighs a deep sigh pretending to be annoyed.

"Aren't you getting too old for this story?" He teases as the lines around his eyes crinkle into a smile. "I've been telling it to you since you were barely potty trained."

"Come on. Please." I whine.

"Once upon a time . . ." He begins as I settle in. "There was a mother and a father who so badly wanted another baby. But they knew they could not get pregnant again. One day they saw an ad for an adoption agency in Atlanta and they knew it was a sign. So they called the agency and ten months later a picture arrived in an email. A picture of a newborn. Brown eyed. Baby girl."

"Me." I sigh into the soft cotton of Papa's shirt.

"And there you were. Our baby girl. We loved you the moment we saw you. We picked you up from the airport six weeks later. Your mother cried when the social worker put you into her arms. She wouldn't let me hold you at first. You were hers. And then you were mine. And you know what kid? You were so small. So small that I could rock you in the palm of my left hand."

"Yeah right!" I roll my eyes. But I watch as Papa picks up his left hand and cups his callused palm and rocks it back and forth. Back and forth in the air.

"Just like this." He says.

And even though I'm too big for fairy tales. Even though tomorrow I face a new school and a new set of 6th grade teachers and a new locker combination. Even though these days I can't help feeling like I'll never be whole. That somewhere out there is a woman with my face. Another mother. Missing me the way I miss her. I try for a moment to imagine what it must have felt like to be so small. To sway and sway and sway. To belong in the cradle of his hand and not fall or blow away like hard dirt in the wind.

El Rio Charter Academy

Is only a mile away from our new house so on Monday Mama and Papa walk us over to register for our first day. El Rio means "the river" and when we arrive I watch a rush of brown and white faces stream out of cars waving goodbye to their parents. But I do not see any faces that look as dark as mine.

In the office the secretary can't stop talking excitedly to us. "Oh my! What an interesting family. So unique. I'm sure the girls will be just fine here. We really are a very diverse school. As you can see we have a very large Latino population. They make up almost fifty percent of the school."

The principal Mr. Bowman takes us on a tour and gives us our locker assignments. My 6th grade classes are all in the main building but Eve gets to be in her own building out back for the high schoolers. We walk across the basketball courts separating the two buildings and Eve nods a quick goodbye before ducking away into her first class.

Then it's just me Principal Bowman and my white white parents standing in the middle of the court. Even though we are all alone I feel like people are watching. I feel like a big smear of color in the middle of a freshly washed sheet.

"Ok sweets." Mama says trying to grab my hand. "Let's get you to your first class."

"Yes. That would be social studies with Mr. Newman." Principal Bowman says leading the way.

And when we get there Mama just can't help herself.

"Anna" Papa starts "let her go in alone. She'll be fine."

But Mama waves him aside and comes into the classroom with me to look around. She watches me take my seat and then she gives me a dorky thumbs-up. She hovers in the doorway as Mr. Newman introduces me. Everyone's eyes are on me. And then they are on Mama. I bury my face in my backpack and pull out my supplies. And I don't take a deep breath until I hear the door shut. Mama's footsteps echoing down the hall.

20 Questions

At lunch a group of 6th grade girls swarm me.

"THOSE are your parents? The ones who dropped you off?"

Yes.

"The white hippie lady with the braid and freckle face? The skinny white dude with the crooked teeth?"

Um yeah . . .

"And that pale girl is your sister too?"

Yeah. Eve. She's in 9th grade.

"So your family's just all mixed up?"

I guess . . .

"So what happened to your real mom?"

You mean my birth mom?

"Did she leave you in a trash can? I heard sometimes babies get left like that."

No . . .

"So those are your stepparents?"

They are my parents.

"So that's your stepsister?"

She's just my sister.

"So why didn't your real parents keep you?"

You mean my birth parents?

"Yeah your real parents."

My "real" parents are my parents. The ones who adopted me.

"Well whatever. What happened to your mom? The one that gave you up?"

I don't really know.

"Why not?"

I had a private adoption. I can't search for her until I'm eighteen.

"That's messed up. But don't you want to know who she is?"

I think so.

"What if she's famous? She could be like Kerry Washington or OPRAH! What if your mom's OPRAH? You'd be so rich."

I . . .

"Ugh. Why do you talk so white?"

This is just how I talk . . .

"Are you sure you're not mixed? You talk too proper to be black."

Well my family is mixed . . .

"So you're like Obama? An Oreo!"

Kinda. Wait. What's an Oreo?

"You know when you're all black on the outside but really white on the inside?"

Um . . .

After lunch even my math teacher Mrs. K has questions.

"So KEE-DAY why don't you stand up and tell us all where you are originally from?"

I'm from here.

"No dear. I mean what country are you from?"

"This one. The good ole U S of A." I say standing up real stiff to give the whole class a fake salute. "And my name is pronounced KAY-DAH."

After School

Eve is waiting for me. She sits on the basketball courts talking to a group of kids in her grade. I watch her exchange phone numbers with some of the girls and they laugh. Already familiar enough to have inside jokes. Making friends is always so easy for her.

Eve sees me standing awkwardly next to her. “Oh hi.” She says. “Ok. See you guys tomorrow. I gotta take this one home.”

“Do you babysit her?” A boy with long hair and a lanky build asks.

Eve laughs. “No. This is my sister.”

“Hi. I’m Keda.” I give a half wave but it’s like he doesn’t even see me.

“Like your cousin-sister? Or like your SIS-TAH?” He continues with a grin.

Eve’s eyes narrow. “No. Like my sister. Like we have the same parents and live in a house together. Ever heard of it?”

“Oh that’s cool. Sorry. Didn’t mean to offend you. I’m all about rainbow families. I have a cousin who is half Jamaican.”

"Good for you." Eve says rolling her eyes. "Let's go." She says to me but I am already walking away.

We walk in silence until we get to the edge of the school property and cut over onto the sidewalk.

"Starting in the middle of the year sucks." Eve finally breaks the silence. "I don't know why we couldn't just stay in Baltimore till school let out. But whatever. At least the kids in my grade are not too bad."

"Yeah." I say. "The girls in my class are ok I think. They ask a lot of questions."

"Yeah. Me too. Did they ask you if you play any sports? I died. I don't think either of our parents have ever picked up any kind of ball. We are so the opposite of an athletic family."

"No. They asked me a lot of questions about being adopted."

"That's kind of personal."

"Yeah. I—"

"Oh my god. Ha! Jasmine just sent me this hilarious gif!"

Eve shoves her phone in my face and I see a flash of a cat flopping dramatically onto a couch with text that reads: I'M LOST WITHOUT YOU.

I MISS YOU TOO B*%#@ She texts back.

Jasmine is Eve's best friend from Baltimore. They met in drama club. I don't really get why they call each other female dogs but Eve tried to explain it to me once. Something about "reclaiming" the word and its power. I watch Eve text back and forth for the rest of the walk. I want to ask her if anyone had questions for her about our family. Or called her a vanilla wafer. But I can tell she's moved on.

Little House on the Prairie

That night before I go to bed Mama comes in to say good night. "So how was your first day?" She asks. "You girls just did your one hour of piano and then disappeared to your rooms after school. And then at dinner you just gave short answers. Did everything go ok?"

"It was fine. Nothing major to report." I say burrowing under the covers. "Where's Papa?"

"He left for rehearsal. He'll be home late and up early for a meeting. But I'm here."

It's hard to tell Mama how I really feel. To explain all the eyes crawling all over me. The questions that never seem to stop. How sometimes I wish I didn't stick out so much. How sometimes I hate her messy hippie braids. How other times I just want to bury my face in their clean shampoo scent. But she looked so worried leaving me earlier that day. Better not to bother her. Mama and I get along so much better when we are lost in a book. Now Mama flips open the page we left off on and begins. Her voice like a swarm of bees lost in the honeysuckle bush.

I fall into a dream of Ma and Pa and Laura and Mary Ingalls

traveling in a big covered wagon across the country. Dreams of my own ma and my own pa and my own sister. The four of us walk through a desert holding hands howling at the moon. Just like a pack of dogs. Together at last. I look up at my dream father and he smiles and then he kisses my dream mother in the silver light and my dream sister squeezes my hand tight. And I know that we will make it after all.

And in the morning when I wake up. I strain my ears for the sound of Pa's voice howling still. The sound of Pa's boots. The sound of Pa Pa Pa. *Oh Pa!* Just ringing through all the sleepiness. I stay very still in my bed praying that this is the day he'll be in the kitchen. Making breakfast. Kissing Mama. "Kid." He'll say. "Forget school. Today is a whole day to spend with just my girls." And then he'll produce a peppermint candy from his pocket that is just for me. And Mama. She will smile. So in love with him. With all of us again.

6th Grade War Games

That's what being at El Rio feels like. One big game. I do my best to write in our notebook and tell Lena all about it.

Wednesday March 16th

Dear L

I've only been going to El Rio for three days and already I can tell there is no one like you here. At lunch today I sat with a few girls but they spoke over me in Spanish and joked about my hummus and turkey sandwich. I don't think they meant to make me feel left out. But I did. Note to self: Learn Spanish.

Then there's Katy. She's white but every day she wears her hair in six messy cornrows. She's always laughing and being followed around by a group of nervous girls. She asks a lot of questions and is always the first to raise her hand in class. Sometimes when I get called on instead I see her eyes narrow.

Today at lunch Katy came up to me and said: "So. You're like really smart huh? That's cool."

What does that even mean? But then she invited me to sit with her and her friends Erica and Ashley. So it wasn't so bad. We watched a few makeup tutorials on her phone and right before the bell rang she took a selfie of the two of us and posted it on Snapchat. I was happy until I saw the caption:

"Hanging out with the whitest black girl I know. <3 < 3"

I know she didn't mean to be rude so I didn't say anything. But I felt really tired after I saw that. My whole body clenched up tight like a fist and stayed like that for the rest of the day.

More soon.

XOXO

K

•••

Monday March 21st

Dear L

Today in gym we had to run ten laps around the basketball court and then play Dribble Mania. Dribble Mania is a stupid game where you have to dribble a ball with one hand and then try to knock someone else's ball out with your free hand. If you lose control of your ball then you're out. Mrs. Drew made us play four rounds and each round I was out in less than a minute.

"Keda!" She yelled at me. "You need to be more focused. Stay low. Watch the ball."

No thanks. I do not need to know how to dribble a ball. I don't even like sports. You know that! Plus. Every time I started to get the hang of it Katy would hunt me down and smack the ball out of my hand.

"I thought you of all people would be good at basketball!" She yelled at me as she ran by.

It was more fun to sit on the sidelines with Amelia. Amelia is shy and quiet but today I learned that she's pretty new to El Rio as well. She moved here from Texas last summer. Amelia has bright green eyes curly brown hair and plump rosy cheeks. She's not very fast on the court either and lives with her mom just down the street from me. We talked about books. It turns out she LOVES the Hunger Games series like we do. And she loves the movies too. I told her we should have movie night to watch them together sometime. She seemed excited about it. I wish you could come too.

XOXO

K

•••

Tuesday March 22nd

Dear L

Katy is really starting to get on my nerves. Today I sat with Amelia at lunch. She was all by herself reading so I joined her. Katy came over like five minutes later and told me that "we needed to talk." Then she told me that I needed to "watch who I hang around with before I get a bad reputation." She said it really loud and I know Amelia heard her. I told her I didn't care and sat back down. She got really mad and leaned in and whisper-oinked in my ear: "Have fun hanging out with the pig."

Can you believe it?! Amelia has curves but she's not a pig. And everyone thinks Katy is so nice.

So I said: "I will." And glared at Katy's back as she walked away. But when I turned around Amelia was gone. She'd left her plate of food and her book open on the table. I found her in the bathroom crying. I tried to comfort her but she just wanted to be left alone. I feel really bad.

I think I've ruined everything.

XOXO
K

•••

Thursday March 24th

Dear L

Today all the girls in 6th grade gave me the silent treatment. I'm pretty sure Katy had something to do with it. When we had to work in groups for social studies nobody would write down my ideas. Amelia was absent so I sat by myself at lunch and wrote this song:

I am not an Oreo
I don't care about basketball
I am smart because I think
I am a girl who likes to read
My hair is strong and all mine

My legs are skinny and defined
I will not be a girl who follows
Or fade away into sorrow
Be free
Be free

What does it mean to be free Lena? I think about this. I do. All the time.

I miss you so much.

XO
K

•••

Sunday March 27th

Dear L

My mom kicked me and Eve out of the house today to "get some air" and "explore." So we walked over to school where some of Eve's new friends were skateboarding. We watched this skinny-looking 10th grader named Trevor tumble down a set of stairs and miss a rail.

Eve laughed at him but then she blushed when he came over to say hi. So gross. I think she likes him.

I was about to yell at her to go when I saw Amelia by the courts. She was with Katy Ashley and Erica of all people! Katy was braiding Amelia's hair into a fishtail and Amelia was smiling.

"Hi Amelia." I said walking up to them. "I didn't know you were going to be here."

Katy smiled sweetly at me. Amelia wouldn't look me in the eyes. Erica and Ashley chewed on their gum and stared past me with empty faces.

"Do you guys hear something?" Katy said.

"Nope." Amelia said too quickly and then giggled.

"Me either. Let's go back to my house. All of a sudden it got really smelly over here."

And so they all got up and ran away from me. Super mature right?

"Ugh she's so awkward." I heard Amelia yell as they left. But then she turned around and mouthed: "I'M SORRY" to me so I know she still likes me.

What's the point of being friends with girls like that? At least I have you and this notebook. And it's already spring break next week so I don't have to deal with any of them for a while.

I can't wait to talk to you on the phone.

XOXO

K

Improvising

On Monday I wake up early but stay in bed reading. Around 10am I hear Papa start to practice his cello in the sunroom. I love waking up to the sound of him playing. Especially when he is playing songs he makes up in his head. Papa sings through his cello. He says it's not really any different than singing with your voice. "You have to breathe with the notes. Inhale at the right moments. Lean into the chords. You have to use your whole body to express the mood and tone of the song." He says.

When I'm making up or improvising songs I try to remember this. I like to stand up in the privacy of my room or outside when I'm alone in nature. I like to scat sing. Like Billie and Ella do with their jazzy voices. I try to imitate different instruments with the sound of my voice. I don't sing any real words. I just open myself to the sounds and sing what I feel. I close my eyes and sway back and forth. I like to think about notes as colors and shapes. I like to swish the notes around in my mouth. Taste them on my tongue. Then I try to fill the whole world with my breath. With my sound.

I get out of bed now and tiptoe into the sunroom. Papa is

facing the big glass windows and dust-filled light floats all around his body. I know he is playing a song he made up because his eyes are closed and the music stand in front of him is empty. I climb onto the futon quietly to listen. He plays for five more minutes and then notices me.

"Good morning my little scoop!" He smiles. "What do you think?"

"I like it. Did you just make it up?"

"I did. Not sure where it's going yet. Do you want to sing along?"

I shake my head.

"I know you can. I hear you in your room sometimes. I see you scribbling lyrics in your songbook."

I shake my head again. "Can you play my song?" I ask instead.

Papa has a song for each of us. Me Mama and Eve. He plays them on our birthdays but sometimes he'll play them on request. He calls my song "the dancing song" because when I was a baby he'd play it and I would giggle and squirm and move around on the sheepskin rug. When I got a little bit older and could walk he'd play it at my birthday parties. Mama would give me scarves and we'd wave them over our heads while skipping and jumping around the room.

"Sure thing kiddo." He says. He lifts his bow dramatically and winks at me before he starts. The whole room fills with an upbeat tune the color of rushing water and sunflowers. I tap my heel in rhythm on the cold tile floors. Then I lift my shoulders up and down a little bit. I bite my lip and shake my head back and forth.

"Come on Makeda!" Papa laughs. "You know you want to dance!"

And I do. It's my song. I get up in my pjs and prance around the room on my tiptoes. I dip and twirl and pretend to wave scarves over my head. Papa laughs and cheers me on and before I know it I start improvising my own song along with the notes.

"Dew-eee-do-do-dat-dat-dat! Weee-weee-da-dat-dat-dat-dat-diddlee-dee-dee!"

I see Mama in the doorway clapping along. I motion for her to join me. And to my surprise she does.

Then we twirl and step and jump and kick in the sunlight just like we used to until we are out of breath. Until Eve walks in and tells us to "KEEP IT DOWN!"

We take one look at her. Her hair bird-nest messy. Drool caked in the corner of her mouth. And we bust out laughing. We keep dancing.

"IT'S NOT FUNNY. SOME OF US ARE TRYING TO SLEEP. IT'S THE FIRST DAY OF SPRING BREAK!" Eve continues.

So Mama and I grab hands and make a circle around Eve. We skip around her until she finally smiles.

"You guys are the worst!" But she flops down on the futon anyway and then Mama and I pile on top of her as Papa finishes my song with a "WHOOP!"

"BRAVO!" We all yell from the futon. Still laughing. All of us awake and alive.

Imagining Mama as a Girl

After our dance party Papa makes buckwheat pancakes and we all sit down together at the table for once. Mama's cheeks are rosy and her eyes glitter with energy. Eve is still grumpy and takes big sips of her orange juice. I grab syrup and butter from the fridge and set it on the table. Mama stands next to Papa at the stove so they are shoulder to shoulder. Almost touching. Mama leans over and kisses Papa on the cheek: "Thank you." She says as he scoops the last pancake onto the waiting plate in her hands.

I drizzle my pancakes with too much syrup and an enormous slab of butter and Mama doesn't even notice. She and Papa sip their tea and share sections of the paper. The table is quiet. But a good quiet. I listen to all of us chewing. The clinking of silverware. The rustling of pages. Even Eve's loud slurping is a comfort. I stuff the three pieces of pancake into my mouth and lean back. And Mama is still reading but I catch Papa sneaking long looks at her from over his glasses. I imagine this is the way he looked at her the first time they met. The first time he saw her in the spotlight. He's told us the story so many times I know it by heart:

Mama walks into the spotlight. She is nineteen. Carnegie Hall is a bowl of tossed sound before her. Her floor-length white gown moves around her legs in rapids.

Onstage she folds then unfolds and refolds the silk scarf she uses instead of a chinrest. She places her violin sharply against her bruised neck. She plucks. Tightens the pegs. Tunes to the oboe's whiny A.

Then closed eyes. A breath. Inhale of rosin. Her body repelling sound like opposite magnets.

And from somewhere. A beginning. First the string section behind her growing louder in her ears. Her fingers stinging as she presses down on the fingerboard waiting for the cue. Then her bow. Flying into the air. Her right arm runaway.

The first note. Hers. Then crescendo. Her whole body singing.

Imagine it. Papa in the cello section. Mama the soloist. All week long for rehearsal she had no idea he was on stage with her. And all week long he had tried to work up the courage to talk to her. And Mama. Nineteen. Playing in front of all those people. She was just a girl. Not much older than me. After the concert Papa (who was just twenty-one himself) found her backstage and asked her out. And here we are now. Eating pancakes. A family full of everyday sounds.

After Breakfast

Papa has a meeting.

"Where's that package you wanted me to drop off at the post office?" He asks me as he packs up his things.

"Oh!" I say. Running to my room. I grab the manila envelope that I've stuffed the purple notebook into with all my letters so far. Lena's address is written on the front in big black letters. "Here." I hand it to Papa back in the kitchen. "It needs to get to Lena ASAP."

Papa adds it to his stack of scores and then stuffs it into his messy bag.

"Don't forget!" I tell him.

"Never." He says earnestly. "I'll make sure to get a tracking number. So you can know exactly where it is and when it will arrive."

"Thanks." I say. Wishing I could go with him to drop it off.

On his way out the door Papa says: "Everyone's going to practice today right?"

Eve and I groan but nod our heads. One hour on the piano. Every day. We know the drill.

"You too love?" Papa looks at Mama. Who is loading up the dishwasher.

"Daniel. Don't start with me." She says. "I don't have any concerts coming up. I'll practice when I have something to practice for."

"I just thought it might feel good. To play. To keep in shape. I know you are still upset about losing that gig in London this winter but . . ."

"I did not 'lose' that gig Daniel! I quit. They were all unprofessional idiots. Amateurs. They didn't know who they were dealing with. My god. I know I don't play as many concerts as I used to but I shouldn't have to promote my own concert. They were doing NOTHING. NOTHING to show they cared."

"Well. I'm not sure that's all true—" Papa tries but Mama cuts him off.

"You're going to be late." Mama slams the dishwasher door. All the color gone out of her face.

Papa gives me and Eve a pained look and slips out into the garage. I hear his Volvo purr awake as he backs out into the driveway and pulls away.

"I'm going to nap." Eve says.

"But you just got up!" I say.

"Yeah. I know. But did I want to get up? No. You guys woke me up with your stomping and your weird gibberish singing."

"It's called jazz. Why don't you ask Siri about it!" I yell after her but she is already halfway down the hallway to her room.

I turn back to Mama. She's staring out of the kitchen window onto the back porch and yard.

"Mama?"

"Yeah?" She says.

"Are you ok?"

"You know. I think I'm going to take a nap too." She says giving me a small smile.

After she leaves I stay in the kitchen and sit at the half-cleared table. Mama has left the book review section open. Her used tea bag wrinkled up on a napkin next to it. Eve's fork is stuck to the table in a pool of syrup. A ring of liquid stares back at me from where Papa's mug sat. It's funny how a house can feel so full one moment. And then completely empty the next. I clear the rest of the table and then head to my room to get dressed. When I walk by Mama and Papa's room. I press my ear to the door and wait until I hear Mama's soft uneven breathing.

Dictionary

There are no more dance parties for the rest of the week. No pancakes. Most mornings Papa is up and out early to record with his chamber music group. Mama gets up to make tea and oatmeal and leaves bowls for me and Eve. By the time we get up she is in her room watching TV. Or sleeping. She gets like this sometimes. Sad. Eve and I know to steer clear of her. "Just give her some space." Papa tells us. "She'll snap out of it eventually. She always does." *But what if she doesn't?* A little voice in my head sings each time she retreats to her room.

On Friday Papa drops us off at the local library so Eve can do research for an English paper she's been avoiding. Of all the sections in the library I love the reference section most. The encyclopedias. The almanacs. The dictionaries are my favorite. I know a lot of words but there are so many I do not know. When I'm here I like to copy at least five new words into my songbook from the Merriam-Webster. At first I had a system to it. Starting with the A's. But after a while I started to play a game instead. I hoist the dictionary off the shelf and find an empty table. Then I sit under the table and put the dictionary out in front of me. I close my eyes and open it to a page. Then I swirl my finger over the open page for seven seconds before letting it fall on a random spot. Whatever word I land on I write down. I do this five times. So many words and each one like a friend.

Luminous (adjective)   giving off a glowing, reflected light

Aperture (noun)—a hole, or space

Jeer (verb)—to taunt or make fun of loudly

Akin (adjective)—blood related, of common ancestry

Cacophony (noun)—a brash, startling sound

I get lost in the words. So lost that the library around me disappears. Then the squat adobe houses surrounding the library. Then the whole simmering city. Until I'm in a forest far away. Surrounded by redwoods and hanging eucalyptus.

"Boo!" Eve pulls me out of my daydreaming. "It's time to go nerd. Step away from the dictionary." She walks away and out the front doors to Papa waiting in the parking lot.

"I'm coming. Stop making such a cacophony." I whisper-yell. But Eve is already gone.

Back to School

That first Monday back I don't even try to make up with Katy and Amelia. I stick to myself and write songs at lunch. Amelia sneaks a look at me as she and the girls walk by to another table but I ignore her. If she wants to be like them that's fine. I am done trying to fit in.

The week is uneventful. I keep to myself. Except for the few times I get to do partner work with this boy Dylan in math class I barely talk to anyone. I walk home after school. I wander around the yard at sunset dreaming of being on my own. I collect rocks on the ditch and visit the bird farm a mile down the road. I sit in the sunroom and write songs about flying. I improvise a world where I am beautiful and strong.

Letters from Lena

By the next Monday all the 6th grade girls seem to have forgotten I exist. And I can't decide if this is better or worse than the silent treatment. Katy has moved on to befriending a new girl named Monica who just transferred from another school over break. And Amelia has been fully absorbed into her crew. Katy doesn't even bother to hunt me down during gym class. But that's fine by me. I have a best friend. It's only been two weeks since I sent Lena the notebook but I'm hoping it comes back to me soon.

I make it through the day as the invisible girl. I get a 95 on my math quiz even though I barely studied for it. After school I walk home. I check the collection of mailboxes at the end of our street but ours is empty. I kick the dirt with my feet as I make my way up the driveway to our house. Eve stayed at school to earn some extra credit and Papa is already gone. Only Mama is home.

I stand outside of the house for a moment. I let the afternoon sun beat down on my face. My neck. I look up at the clear blue sky and then back at our house. It stares back at me with its empty-eyed windows. I can already feel Mama's cloudy mood hanging over it. When I get inside I check on Mama. But she is not in her room. She is not in the sunroom or the living room or the kitchen.

"Hello?" I call out. But I am met with silence. I clench my teeth.

I check the garage. Mama's van sits quietly in the dark heat. I relax my jaw. *She's not gone. She's just on a walk or something. She'll be home soon.*

Back in the kitchen I notice a package on the table. "Lena!" I yell out loud. I tear it open. And out falls our notebook. I grab an apple from the counter and then run into the sunroom. Then I sit down and read each of her letters as fast as I can.

Friday April 1st

Dear K

OMG I was too excited to get home from gymnastics tonight and get our notebook!!! I grabbed it from my dad who was sorting the mail on the kitchen table and then ran upstairs to my room. My dad was like "Not even a hello from you? How was your day?" And I was like "NOPE!" I tore the envelope open before I even could get my backpack and shoes off. Then I read all of your letters. Twice.

Keda. What do you mean the houses in Albuquerque are made of mud? Is that safe? I can't imagine living in a house like that. Sounds cool. Also. I thought of a new nickname for you #10bottlesaday. Because that's how much lotion it sounds like you need in that desert. But you know we can be #ashyforlife together since our moms only want to buy us that nasty organic stuff that doesn't even work on our skin. I'll send you a bottle of Jergens if you send me one.

ANYWAY.

What IS the boy situation at El Rio? You write a lot about the girls at your new school. They sound evil. But more importantly please tell me about the boys. LOL. I know. I'm obsessed. But I dumped Damian. (That white boy with the big ears we met at the pool last summer?) We only went out (secretly) for a couple weeks. But then we were at the park and he pulled on the root of my braid and asked how it stayed in so well. Tried to tell me he thought it was ok to touch my hair because "I'm not like the other black girls" he's met before. "You know." He said: "You seem more white." BOY BYE.

I'M NOT WHITE. THAT'S JUST MY PARENTS.

Why does nobody understand this? Mom's calling me for dinner. More soon! So soon. I miss you.

Your BFF
L

•••

Sunday April 3rd

Dear K

Today after church I told my parents I didn't want to go anymore. They said I'm too young to make that decision for myself. It made me so mad that I burst into tears.

It's not that I don't believe in god. You know I do. But I don't think my parents understand that it's not about that. You know when grown-ups say something to you they THINK is a compliment but it's really not? That happens to me all the time at church. I can't take it anymore. Like last week. Jax our youth group leader was telling us about all the "poor kids" in the third world and how we need to be grateful for what we have and give back to those in need. And then he looked right at me and said: "Right Lena? I'm sure you're grateful that your parents decided to save you through adoption." I got up and went to the bathroom so nobody would see how upset I was. It reminded me of how Katy made you feel when she called you "the whitest black girl." Forget her. And forget Jax.

Have you only been gone a month? It feels like forever. I have one more week of school before my Spring Break. Maybe I'll get on a bus and come visit you? Just kidding. (Kinda.)

Your BFF

L

•••

Tuesday April 5th

Dear K

I went outside and sat under our willow today after school. The leaves are starting to bud. It was weird without you. Are there willow trees in Albuquerque? Probably not. I am trying to make new friends at school. I mean. I've always been school friends with Rebecca Julie and Safiya. We've known each other since kindergarten. But we don't hang out much outside of school. That was always you and me time.

Can I tell you a secret? I was kind of

jealous reading about Amelia at first. I thought maybe she might replace me. I know that's dumb. Because. You know. I'm one of a kind! LOL. But it's hard to think that you might find another best friend.

Dunno. I am blah today. And reading about how Amelia turned on you made me extra mad. Katy is a monster. Stay away from her. She's not worth your time. If she was a real friend she'd know you may not be good at basketball but you sing like a queen.

Your BFF
L

•••

Wednesday April 6th

Dear K

Spring Break tomorrow! Wahoo! My mom is taking me to DC in the morning. Just for a few days. I even get to take a break from gymnastics. We're going to the National Museum of African American History and Culture. My mom is so excited we finally got tickets. She has like a whole plan written out. I guess I'm excited too. I hear they have good food in the cafeteria. And that they have a whole exhibit about black athletes. I'm trying to be in a museum one day. You know what I'm saying? Right next to Simone Biles and Gabby Douglas. They also have an exhibit called "Musical Crossroads" all about black music and traditions. I told my mom we have to go to that one too so I can take pictures for you. You know they have some of Billie Holiday's master records on display? I wish you could come with us.

Anyway. Before we leave tomorrow I'm going to mail the notebook back to you. I know I haven't even had it that long but I can't wait to get it back from you again. It should get to you in the next 3-4 days. WHEN YOU GET IT HURRY UP AND WRITE AND TELL ME EVERYTHING. I miss you SOOOOOO much. Don't ever forget that I am your #ashyforlife bestie and I will fight Katy (with my words) to defend your honor. You are a queen. A QUEEN I tell you.

Your BFF
L

I read Lena's letters again. I giggle and let her words warm my chest. *I am a queen.* And then I feel a tightness in my ribs when I think about Lena alone. Under our willow. I look outside of the sunroom windows. I scan our dry and patchy lawn. The one gnarly cottonwood tree that provides shade over the back fence and ditch looks pathetic in comparison to the delicate lace arms of the willow tree. But before I can even start to cry I see a small movement in the backyard. Mama. She is sitting on a chair in the lawn. Close to the porch door. She stares at the ditch. A collection of tissues next to her in the grass creates a little mountain. And she picks and picks and picks at the dry skin on her naked heels. She does not see me. And I do not tell her I am here. I just stay in the sunroom. Holding on to Lena's warm words. Watching Mama until she finally comes inside and starts dinner.

In the Locker Room

That Wednesday. After gym. Katy decides to talk to me again. She comes up to me and pokes at my belly and laughs. "You need to do some ab work." I quickly put on my shirt and jeans and stuff my gym clothes into my bag. I know Katy is mad that her team lost the kickball game. Even madder that I was the one to score the final point. I may not be good at kicking the ball. At catching the ball. Or even understand all the rules of the game but I do know how to run. And that's what I did. The bases loaded. Me on first. And when this kid Sammy kicked the ball all the way into the outfield I ran my butt off. Sliding into home base just before Katy. Who was stationed there as catcher. Could get me out.

Now she's being a sore loser and I'm going to be late for math. I try to leave the locker room but Katy blocks my way. Amelia Erica and Ashley are behind me. Still getting dressed but I feel their eyes glued on us.

"Is this your hair?" Katy is in my face now. Her hands picking at my locs one by one.

"Yeah. It's mine."

"So you're sure it's not a weave?"

"No. It's my hair. And so what if it was a weave?"

"How come you never wash it? I mean you always wear that plastic cap in the shower."

"I do wash it. At home. I just don't need to wash it every day. My hair is different from yours."

"Ew gross." I hear Erica giggle.

Katy ignores her. But leans in. "You should really keep that to yourself."

"What?"

"That you don't shower every day."

"But that's not what I said. I shower. I just don't wash my hair every day."

"Whatever. Just trying to give you some advice. You don't want everyone in school to think you're a dirty nigger do you?"

I hear Amelia suck in the air behind me. But then there is silence.

"Oh you know what I mean. You just don't want to be like those ghetto girls. Just a pro tip from me to you." Katy says with a smile. Untangling her pointer finger from one of my locs before returning to her locker. "Besides. You want to smell good for Dylan don't you? I see how you look at him in class. You think he's cute."

I am frozen. And even though I just showered I feel like my skin is crawling.

"Katy." I hear Amelia say with a shaky voice. "You can't say that word."

"Well I just did. Plus Keda's cool. She's not like other black people. She knows what I mean."

I don't know what she means. I am sweating. My tongue feels swollen. I feel tears building in the corners of my eyes. Nobody has ever said that word to me. So I do the only thing I can do. I run. Out of the locker room. Down the hall. Until I make it to math. Then I wipe my face. And slip into the room.

"Keda. You're late. That's a warning. Sit down please." Mrs. K says. But I barely hear her or anything else for the rest of the day.

Blackmail

After school I rush out of the building hoping to avoid Katy but she's waiting for me on the basketball courts. When she sees me she throws her arm around my shoulders and says: "Walk with me."

Maybe she is going to apologize? For a moment her arm around my shoulders feels light and warm. Not hard and unmoving like it did in the locker room.

"Listen. We're cool right?" She starts. "I mean. I was just joking. You're not mad are you? Sometimes I just say stupid things. But it doesn't mean anything."

"But it does." I hear myself say. "It does. You know I'm black right?"

"I mean I have eyes. But you're not like regular black people. You're the—"

"The whitest black girl you know!" I say taking the words right out of her mouth. "I know! I know. I wish you'd stop saying that."

"Listen. Are you going to make this a bigger deal than it is?"

"What do you mean?"

"I mean are you going to report me or something."

"I dunno."

"Well." She starts her arm getting tighter around my neck. "I hope not. Because if you do I'll tell the whole school who you like."

"I don't know what you're talking about. Please let go of me." I say. "I want to be alone."

"Promise me that you won't say anything. Or else the whole school will know about your crush."

"Fine. Whatever. I won't tell. Just leave me alone please."

"Sure thing. See ya friend."

"You're not my friend." I tell her.

But Katy is already skipping off in the opposite direction. I wait for Eve to get out but remember she is staying after for drama club. So I walk home alone. Kicking the road as I go.

I Do Have a Crush

On Dylan. He has bright red hair and freckles all over his nose. He sits in front of me in math class and once during partner work he let me borrow a pencil. He has sea-green eyes and he likes to play pranks on other boys in our grade. This week he covered the toilets in the boys' bathroom with Saran wrap. The week before that he Post-it bombed his friend Brian's locker. He pretends like he's dumb but he's not. I watch him speed through math problems. When he gets his papers back they always have A's on them. And he helps me with my work sometimes. Today he caught me staring at him and winked at me. I hid my face in my book for the rest of the class.

I call Lena when I get home. And she picks up this time.

"Keda!" She screams into the phone. "Where have you been all my life!"

"In hell." I joke. And we both laugh.

I instantly feel calmer. My skin stops crawling and my heart slows down. It is so good to hear a familiar voice.

"So." She says. "Did you get my letters?!"

"YES! I read them so fast. You dumped Damian? LOL. You were too good for him anyway."

"You know it. Anyway. How's that Katy girl? Do I need to come fight her?"

"Maybe." I say. But I don't want to talk about Katy. Or about what she said. "Lena. You know you won't fight anybody."

"True. But you KNOW I can take down someone with my words. Easy."

"I know."

"And boys?" Lena can tell I want to move on. "Any boyfriend potential?"

"Maybe. I guess."

"You guess? Come on Keda. Tell me. Tell me now."

It feels good to think about something other than what happened in the locker room. It's embarrassing. I normally tell Lena everything. But this feels different. Like if I speak it out loud it's somehow more real. So I tell Lena all about Dylan instead. Every small detail about his freckles and pranks and how he leans back in his desk chair and laughs. I tell her about the Friday night mixer coming up. About how I wish he'd ask me.

"Well why don't you ask him?" She interrupts.

"What if he says no?"

"Well then he's not worth your time."

"I don't know. I'm not sure if he likes girls like . . . us. You know?" I say.

"Oh you mean he's racist? Well then if that's true he's definitely not worth your time. But I bet he thinks you're cute. He winked at you remember? He gave you HIS pencil. Those seem like signs to me."

"I dunno."

We start talking about something else. By the time we finish catching up it's time for dinner. Lena and I say goodbye and promise to talk again soon. I don't tell her about the word I was called. I just want to pretend it never happened.

There Are Terrible Songs in Me

Songs buried in the ditch of my mind. Songs tangled in my throat. Forgotten melodies. I am sleepless again. So I look up the word that night in my dictionary. I am looking for a way out of it. I know the word. But I have never been the word. Now the *gg* so close together on the page looks like bars I cannot get my arms through.

Nigger (noun)

An offensive word for a black person

A dark-skinned person

A person who is part of a people who are systematically discriminated against and receive unfair treatment

I know I am not stupid. That I am not dirty. That I wash myself every day. That my skin needs the lotion I slather on each morning greasing my elbows the back of my knees. "This is me. Me." I whisper into the dark of my room but there are terrible songs in me. Songs full of minor chords and shattering notes.

When I open my mouth I am ashamed of my own voice breaking in half. I am ashamed of the way I smell. Like an overripe piece of fruit. I curl into the nest of my bed. I curl and curl and curl. Trying to defend myself against the desert cold that seems to have seeped in through every crack in my room.

I Start to Question

If it ever happened at all. But at lunch the next day I cannot eat a thing. My stomach seesaws at the smell of grease and burnt cheese wafting from the kitchen. My hummus and turkey sandwich gets stuck in my throat and I have to take a big swig from my water bottle to get it to go down. The cafeteria is business as usual. A room of harsh sound and blinding fluorescent light. I watch Katy saunter in and load her tray with pepperoni pizza. And Ashley and Erica follow suit. Amelia looks enviously at their trays as she fills hers with a single apple and some iceberg lettuce.

It was not a joke. Not to me. My stomach flip-flops as I remember how easily she said it. How the whole locker room echoed with the word. How everyone must have heard it. My face boils as they walk up and sit down next to me not making eye contact. As if I don't exist. No regard for what Katy has done or said. *Oreo. The whitest black girl.* All of these were names I could endure. But not this one. She cannot get away with this one.

I throw my sandwich in the trash and storm outside. Mrs. Drew is setting up cones for the 7th graders on the field. Some stupid obstacle course they'll no doubt have to navigate with a soccer ball.

"What can I do for you Keda?" She starts. "You're supposed to be at lunch."

"I need to report hate speech."

"Well that's a little dramatic. Are some of the girls giving you a hard time? I assure you we take bullying very seriously here."

"No. It was hateful. Katy used the N-word when we were in the locker room yesterday after gym. To my face."

I watch Mrs. Drew's back stiffen. She starts to fiddle with a cone. Moving it to the left and then the right even though the field is pretty much set up.

"I see." She says after a long minute. "Well are you sure you heard right? There was a lot of yelling and excitement at the end of that game that carried into the locker rooms. I'm sure none of our students would use that word. I would have heard if someone used that word."

This was a mistake. I can see it on her face. She doesn't want to deal with this today. Or any day. Mrs. Drew can't even remember the names of all the students in her classes. A really nice white lady who doesn't want to be bothered with any mess.

"Never mind. Forget it." I say my shoulders full of knots.

"Well now if I hear it again I'll shut it down. But if nobody else heard it I can't do anything."

"People heard." I say walking away now. "People heard."

Saturday April 16th

Dear L

I have to tell you something. I've been keeping it in all week. I can't sleep. I keep replaying what happened in my head over and over. I think you are maybe the only person who will understand.

What's the worst name you've ever been called?

On Wednesday. After gym. Katy got in my face and warned me not to be a "dirty N-word." I didn't tell you on the phone because I wanted to forget it. But I can't.

Why does telling the truth never work? I tried to speak up for myself. I went to my gym teacher the next day and told. But Mrs. Drew just said that I must have "heard wrong" because she didn't hear it.

Can you believe it?! Adults never listen. I did NOT hear wrong. But nobody else will say anything. Not Amelia. Not Ashley or Erica. So it's my word against Katy's. And who is gonna listen to me? I am so angry I could punch someone. I am so tired I could sleep for the rest of the weekend.

I'm gonna just stick to myself from now on. And I'm definitely not telling anyone in my family. Can you imagine? My mom would die. She'd probably cry about it for days. No. I just want to bury this. Deep.

XOXO
K

PS I'm going to ask Dylan to the mixer next week. Why not. Before it's too late. Thanks for the pep talk.☺

The Friday Mixer

Is three days away. It's now or never. On Tuesday I wait for Dylan after school by the front entrance. He comes bursting out of the school doors with a group of friends.

"Hey!" I manage to squeak out before he passes me. "Can I talk to you?"

"Oh. Hey Keda." He says. "What's up?"

"Um. I just. I just wanted to say thanks. Thanks for letting me use your pencil that one day."

"Oh. Ok. Yeah. No problem. Is that it?"

"Yes. I mean no. Um. Are you going to the Friday mixer?"

"Yeah. Katy asked me. We're going together. I guess. Listen. I have to go. My parents are waiting. See you tomorrow ok?"

"Ok." I squeak as I watch him run and jump into a red car that seems to match the autumn red of his hair. "No problem."

But it is a problem. I am beginning to think I might actually be invisible. *Of course Katy asked him. She knew I liked him.* I am in a bad mood for the rest of the afternoon. I stomp home and run into the bathroom. I study my face. And yank apart the locs at the back of my head that have started to grow together. I yank so hard that I pull a few of them out entirely. I throw them into the toilet and flush. They swirl to the bottom and are gone. Then I just stand there. Staring at the empty toilet. Wishing I could disappear too.

Questions I Have for Black Girls Like Me

Who loves us?

Who wants to dance with us?

Who sees us?

Who understands us?

Who holds us?

Who thinks we are beautiful?

We love you baby girl

The Georgia Belles sing back

We dance with you

We see you growing

We understand you

We can hold you

You are more beautiful

Than midnight

Maps

On Thursday I am in first period social studies taking a geography quiz on the countries of West Africa when I hear my name on the loudspeaker: "Makeda Kirkland please report to the main office."

Accra Ghana

Monrovia Liberia

Dakar Senegal

I fill in the names of countries and their capitals as fast as I can onto a blank map. I know I am good at geography. Tracing boundaries of faraway places with my fingers. Learning small facts about each one. Holding those facts on my tongue. I trace my fingers over the African countries and wonder if I am part of this history. Where I came from. Where my people came from. In the beginning. Before I was even born.

Where are you really from? People always ask me. And I say: *Here. America.* Because it's true. But I know there is more to my story. My birth mother's story. I am like this blank map. Trying to name itself.

"Makeda Kirkland please report to the main office."

Freetown Sierra Leone

I scribble my final answer and then pack up my things. When I hand in my quiz Mr. Newman gives me a small tight-lipped smile and says: "That was quick."

When I get to the main office Mama is there in her sweatpants and a stained sweatshirt. At least her braids are neat and she appears to be wearing a bra. Eve is also in the office. Sitting in a chair in the corner of the room. Her face full of edges. She glares at Mama and then me as I enter.

"You ruin EVERYTHING." Eve yells as she slumps further into the chair and starts madly texting on her phone. I can't tell if she's talking to me or Mama. Or both of us.

I look back at Mama and realize that she is holding my notebook. OUR notebook. The one that belongs to Lena and me.

"Makeda." She starts. Shaking her head. "I'm sorry but what happened in gym last week is unacceptable. Why didn't you tell me?! I'm taking action. I'm pulling you girls out of this school. You will not be attending El Rio anymore."

"That's private." I manage to say. Pointing at the notebook in her hands.

But Mama has turned away from me and is yelling at the principal now. Something about their "incompetent teaching staff." How no daughter of hers will be part of a school that "condones the use of oppressive language. A school that cannot see past color and difference and accept all its students as human."

She is making a scene. And the room is so full of her. I get lost. I can't breathe. I can't even see straight through my tears. Why is she so angry? Is she crying too? Why is she crying? This happened to me. Not her. And those are my words. My words. Not hers.

The Short Drive Home

Is silent at first. Mama tries to catch my eye in the rearview but I look out the window instead. I stare directly at the sun for as long as I can until my eyes burn and small black dots dance through my blurry vision.

"Girls." Mama says from up front. "I know you hate me right now. But this is for the best. That school wasn't teaching you anything anyway."

"How do you know!" Eve yells. "I had friends there!"

"Well you can still see those friends. On weekends if you like."

"Not the same. And what. Are you just going to put us in another school?" Eve continues. "It's almost summer. There's only a month and a half left! You can't keep doing this. Just because you quit every job you ever get doesn't mean we have to do the same. You never think ANY school is good enough for us."

"No. No more school. I'm going to teach you at home. Like I always should have." Mama says. Her teeth clenched.

"Oh great." Eve rolls her eyes. "That's going to be so fun. I just don't understand why WE are being punished for some racist thing another girl said. It's not fair."

Mama and Eve continue to argue while I remain quiet in the back. This isn't the first time she's taken us out of a school. Back in Baltimore we were on our third school in four years. I loved the public Montessori we went to but all of a sudden when I was in 4th grade and Eve in 7th Mama claimed they were "too unstructured." For my 5th grade year and Eve's 8th grade year we were at a Catholic school with uniforms. But when Mama found out I had sat through a sex education course that preached "abstinence only" she cussed out our principal at the end-of-year picnic. So. We didn't go back. So that's when Mama sent us to our local public school. But we only made it halfway through the year before we moved. And now. Here we are. Again.

Something happens to me and somehow the two of them become the loudest.

I look up front. Mama and Eve both have flushed cheeks. Small strands of their thick brown hair break free and crown their faces. I notice they have the same light freckles on their moonstone arms. I look at my own reflection in the rearview mirror. My round face. My dark brown eyes. My skin the color of ditch water. Muddy river. *One of these things just doesn't belong.* I think. And I pick at the dry skin on my elbow. Pick and pick and pick until it stings.

"Makeda?" Mama is speaking to me now. "I'm sorry I read your notebook to Lena. I was worried about you. You're so quiet these days. So private. And that word you were called. My god. I can't believe people are still using that word. It's shocking! Your gym teacher should have gotten that girl expelled. Are you ok?"

I nod quickly and turn back to the window. There's no trying to argue with Mama. When she's like this it's better just to let it go. And maybe she's right. *What was I learning at that school anyway?*

The sun is turning into a blood-orange ball in the sky. I wonder what it feels like to be the sun. To be that hot and full of fire. I wish Mama had just asked me how I was feeling. Or at least come to me first instead of making a huge scene like she always does. I wish she hadn't ruined the one place it felt safe to be me.

Questions for HER

Where were our ancestors from?

Do you dream about the ocean?

Do you have nightmares about the ocean?

Did anyone ever call you the N-word?

What do you keep for yourself?

Where do you go to be free?

Why did you give me up?

Where are you now?

Where are you?

Betrayed

"Something happened."

"Keda. Tell me now. What's going on?" Lena says.

I am in my room inside my closet with my papa's cell phone. Mama and Papa are still yelling in the living room. *How could you make a decision like that without me! Pulling them BOTH out of school. Again! There are other ways we could have dealt with this. You've got to stop making irrational decisions like this. It's getting out of hand Anna. I don't like what happened to Makeda either. But we've got to take the time to talk about these things. Before you act.* Papa had exploded a few hours earlier at dinner. And Mama had exploded right back at him.

They've been arguing for hours. But besides Mama asking me if I was ok in the car nobody has come to talk to me.

"Keda. You're scaring me. Are you there?"

"Yeah." I say. "I'm here. I just needed to hear your voice."

"Is it your mom again?"

"Kinda."

"Is it that witch Katy? I'll kill her."

"You're not going to kill anybody." I laugh then. Letting a few tears loose down my face.

"Then what is it?!"

"My mom read our notebook. ALL OF IT." The words come tumbling out. "And there was a letter to you. About something Katy said to me in the locker room last week. So my mom pulled us out of school and now everybody in my house is angry. And it's my fault."

"Wait. Slow down. So no school just for a little while or like forever?"

"Forever. Like Eve and I are not going back to El Rio. Or any school. At all. All because Katy called me a . . ."

"A what?!"

My throat feels like it's being strangled by a thick rope. "I didn't want to talk about it. I wrote you about it. But I just wanted to forget it." I manage to get out.

Lena is quiet on the other line. We breathe together for a minute and it calms me down. Then after a beat she says. "Did she call you the N-word?"

"Yeah." I squeak. *Why am I trembling?*

I wait for Lena to yell. But she is silent. "Are you still there?" I ask.

"Yes."

"Are you mad?"

"Yes."

"I am sorry." I say. "It's all my fault. I should have hidden the notebook better." Tears are streaming down my face but I'm trying not to snot all over the phone.

"I'm not mad at you." Lena finally says. "I just . . . Well I've never been called that word to my face. But hearing that you have kind of feels like I have too. You know? Like someone punched us both in the gut."

"Yeah."

"Listen." Lena says then. "Don't worry about the notebook. You're still my BFF. Ok? And I still want to hear everything that's happening in your life."

"Me too." I squeak again. "But I don't think writing each other is safe anymore. Maybe we can email instead?"

"This is so unfair!" Lena yells. Finding the strength in her voice again. "Your mom and Katy can't ruin the notebook for us! Listen. I have to go. I have a meet. But I have an idea. Check your email tomorrow ok? When nobody is around."

"Ok."

"And Keda?"

"Yeah?"

"I'm sorry. I am sorry she said that to you."

And hearing Lena apologize for something neither of us did sets all my tears free.

Sisters

Are forever. That's what the picture frame Eve gave me last Christmas says around the edges. Inside the frame is a picture of me and Eve from the day I arrived. I am just a baby. Six weeks old with a head of fluffy rain-cloud hair. Kola nut brown eyes. Blackberry puckered lips. I am wearing a tiny yellow onesie and Eve is holding me softly in her lap. Eve is three and a half. She's all dressed up in a pink and black polka dot dress. Her hair shoved into two thick pigtails with a shiny silver bow on each one. I love this picture because normally when there's a camera present Eve cannot help herself. She poses. Flirts. Flips her hair and smiles directly into it. "Puts the cheese all the way on." Papa likes to say. "Like a true diva." But in this picture she has forgotten all about the camera. She is looking down at me in her lap. She is not smiling but her face is full of light. She's looking down at me and her lips are slightly parted as if she's whispering a secret to me. And only me. I keep the photo on my dresser. Next to my collection of angel figurines and a small wire tree full of necklaces and earrings.

Sisters are forever. But is Eve still mad at me? After I get off the phone with Lena I knock softly on her door and enter. Eve is on her bed. Lying on top of a collection of magazines. Clothes and tissues. I can tell she's been crying.

"Hey." I offer. "This sucks huh?"

"Yeah. It does. I was really starting to enjoy school you know?"

I don't know exactly. Everything about El Rio was exhausting to me. But I do know what it's like to feel like you're missing out. That your friends are far away.

"Why didn't you tell me?" Eve continues. "I could have handled those girls on my own. The ones that were messing with you."

"Dunno. Guess I thought it was just best to let it go."

"But that's really messed up. Keda. What she said to you. How can you just let that go? You should have said something. It affects me too you know."

"I did—"

"You can't just let people walk all over you like that."

"I didn't—"

"Anyway. Whatever. This year has been a waste. Soon as June hits I'm getting a job. No way I'm homeschooling all through May and staying in this house all summer with Mama."

I shuffle my feet awkwardly inside the doorway. I wish she would invite me onto her bed like she used to. I feel like there's a big canyon between us. I yell something into the canyon and it echoes across to her but only half the message gets there. She yells back and it's the same.

What's the worst name you've ever been called? I want to ask her. But I decide against it. Instead I say: "I'm sorry." Even though I haven't done anything wrong.

"It's not really your fault." Eve says starting to text someone. "It's just messed up that we have to live like this."

We? I think.

"Yeah." I say. "It is."

The Georgia Belles

Will not let me sleep

Or maybe I am keeping myself up

I can't stop thinking about HER

My birth mom

I want her here

And I don't

I want to crawl into her lap

And I want to push her away

Baby girl baby girl

The Belles sing

You are stuck deep in this mud

Dig dig dig yourself out

I am not a baby girl

I am not your baby girl

I am full of spores and seeds

Bursting in the wind

I want to be everywhere

And nowhere all at once

I want to be a blank map

A map full of space

Where do I go

With this name of mine?

This name

I have been called?

You go on you go on

Dig dig dig the Belles answer

All through the night

Our Bodies Ourselves

The day after Mama pulls us out of school she wakes us up early and takes us to the bookstore. "This is not going to be 24/7 vacation." She says as we walk through the glass doors into the store. She's wearing a plain but clean long sleeve shirt. Jeans. Her braids pinned around her head in a crown. She has a notepad full of lists: Books. Websites. Phone numbers. "I stayed up late last night thinking this through and convincing your father that this is the best way. We are going to make these last five weeks of the school year count!" She continues.

"So what's the plan?" Eve asks yawning. Her eyes already scanning the magazine aisle.

"You each are to pick out two books. One nonfiction book about a period in history you're interested in. One book of fiction. Classic or contemporary. And I'm going to pick up some AP English books for Eve and look at the curriculum aisle."

"What about math and science?" I ask.

"Well. You know I'm not really strong in those areas. So I'm looking into some groups and online classes for you. Today let's focus on history and literature."

"No offense." Eve says. "But how are you going to teach us everything we need to know when you barely graduated high school?"

"Eve." Mama lets out a long sigh. "You know that school is just another oppressive capitalist institution right? And even more so these days with all that standardized testing and Common Core crap. I want you to be independent thinkers. And no. I didn't go to college and I barely finished high school. But you know what? The world gave me an education! I traveled to six of the seven continents before I was seventeen because of my career. I've learned a lot from the people I played music with. Who hosted me in their homes and took me around their cities. And from books. And the internet. You can learn anything you want these days on the internet. So please. Just approach this as an adventure. Where you get to decide what questions to ask and what interests you! Don't you want to take control of your own destiny?"

"God. Don't get all preachy on us. We get it." Eve rolls her eyes. "I just think we could have at least finished this year at El Rio. You know. But whatever. Let's have an adventure. Sounds super fun." Eve splits off and heads to the drama section.

"How are you doing today peach?" Mama looks at me now. "Still mad at me too?"

"No. Just tired." I say. And it's not a lie. I'm exhausted by Mama's sudden energy. How long is this going to last? The first couple weeks after we moved Mama was up every day getting boxes unpacked. Barking orders. Putting together the house. And then she just stopped. Stopped getting dressed. Stopped caring. Will this be the same?

For my history book I pick out a book about the Civil Rights Movement. It has lots of pictures and time lines. Then I move to the fiction section. The classics. I pick out a book called *The Bluest Eye* by Toni Morrison.

When we're ready to check out Mama stacks our books together. And then on top she places a huge book called *Our Bodies, Ourselves*.

"Are you serious?" Eve says. "That book is huge."

"Right. And it has *everything* you girls will ever need to know about women's health. It's a feminist classic. You read this and you will know everything you need to know about your bodies. Better than any sex education or health class you'd get at school."

"Ha!" Eve says. "I doubt that."

"Well. I wish my mom had made me read this when I was your age. I will not have girls who don't understand how their uteruses work."

"Shhhh! Why are you yelling?"

"Oh come on! *Uterus* is not a bad word. Neither is *vagina*. VAGINA. VAGINA. Say it with me girls." Mama yells.

"That will be $111.50." The guy ringing us up behind the counter interrupts.

And Eve and I stand behind Mama. Mortified. As he takes Mama's credit card. And Mama just stands there. Oblivious.

Top Secret

Later that afternoon I hop on the desktop computer in the sunroom that Eve and I use for homework sometimes. It's pretty slow but Eve and I can at least get on the internet. Mama has a laptop but she says it's off-limits to us. Even though she barely even uses it. I log into my email and the first thing I see is a message from Lena.

April 22
From: LenaBeans@gmail.com
To: JazzyK@gmail.com
SUBJECT: Top Secret

Dear K
I set up a Tumblr for us. If we set our posts to private only the two of us can see it. Let's post each other letters on there ok? We just need a good name for the blog that no one will guess. I'll

let you pick that. You're much better with words than I am.

Remember. You are my BFF. I want to know EVERYTHING that happens to you. Even when it's hard.

To log in:
Username: LenaBeans@gmail.com

I'm not going to write the password here. But here is a clue I think you'll get

#ashyforlife

I can't wait for your first post.
Your BFF
L

I am smiling so big the corners of my lips hurt. It's genius. Our own Tumblr! I quickly listen for any movement in the house. But Mama is in her room sleeping and Eve walked over to El Rio about an hour ago to whine to her friends about the unfairness of life. Papa as usual is at work. I type in the login information and then I stare at the blinking cursor in the password box. *#ashyforlife?* I type in JERGENS. Denied. I try ASHYQUEENS. Denied. I type #10BOTTLESADAY and "I'm in!" I whisper.

It takes me less than five minutes to set up our theme and upload a picture of the two of us. Then I add our title and tagline:

QUESTIONS I HAVE FOR
BLACK GIRLS LIKE ME

"I'm not white. That's just my parents."

Letters between #ashyforlife adopted besties.

posted April 22nd

Dear L

This is the best thing that has happened to me ALL year. I hope you like the title I made up. And for my first post here are some QUESTIONS I HAVE FOR BLACK GIRLS WHO HAVE BEEN CALLED NAMES:

What's the worst name you've ever been called?
How do you forget it?
What makes you angry?
What makes you feel powerful?

Who sees you the most?

What does love feel like?

To me. Love feels like having a best friend.

XOXO

K

Chicks

The next morning Mama decides to start a farm on our half acre of land. "Taking care of animals will teach us all some important skills!" She says turning the lights in our rooms on at 6am. We drive along the dark pebbly streets until the land bleeds with sunrise. An hour later we arrive at a feed shop. Outside is a chalkboard that reads CHICKS FOR SALE. ONE DOZEN FOR $10. I still have sleep in my eyes but I wipe them quickly when I see Mama emerging from the shop carrying a medium-sized cardboard box. She puts the box between me and Eve on the middle back seat and we peer in. Twelve yellow chicks with sleep still in their eyes too are peeping and pooping and squatting in the corners.

"Soon we'll have fresh eggs." Mama says starting the engine. "Soon."

I take one of the chicks up in my hands. Hold it just tight enough to feel its fragile ribs. I feel like god. Creator. I squeeze just enough until it stops squirming and then release it wiggling and breathing again. I kiss its iridescent beak and put it back in the box. Then I repeat again and again with each chick. *Reach. Squeeze. Kiss. Reach. Squeeze. Kiss.* Until we are home.

New Routines

It turns out it takes six months for baby chicks to grow into hens that lay eggs. For the next couple of weeks Eve and I get used to our new routine at home. At first Mama wakes us up at 8am but soon we're rolling out of bed at 10am. We eat oatmeal or granola and then take turns raising up our new pets. I don't mind the baby chicks. They are cute and fluffy and fragile. The chicks are not big enough to be in the coop yet. So we keep them in a corner of the garage penned in with a wire gate with heat lamps clamped to it to make sure they don't get cold or sick. We have to change their water often. And leave chick feed scattered around so they can eat and grow big and strong. Most of the chicks are yellow with a little bit of brown. Like bananas ripening in the sun. Mama says that when they get older they will start to change color and we'll be able to tell them apart better. For now I call them all "Angel" because when they huddle close together they look like a glowing ring of light. Like a halo.

I feel important being in charge of the chicks. I think Eve does too. Because even though she complains about the smell or how we have to keep changing the newspaper in their pen when it gets too full of poop. She always reminds me when it's my turn to check on them. Even though she knows I never forget. And sometimes she comes into the garage with me just so she can play with them some more.

Other than checking on the chicks every few hours the days pass slowly. Besides trips to the library and weekly piano lessons with our new teacher Mrs. Umanski. Mama lets us make our own schedules.

"I want you both to finish the books I bought you by the end of the month. Then we'll have a discussion about what you learned. If you encounter a word you don't know underline it and then look it up! That way you have an ongoing vocabulary list."

Usually after breakfast I sit in the sunroom with a roll of highlighters and my book. I'd rather watch TV but the only one we have is in Mama and Papa's room and we're not allowed to watch it unless she invites us. I find other ways to pass the time. I try to read two chapters a day. One from each of my books. Then I spend time on the desktop computer. I write Lena on our blog when no one is around. Eve is more of a night owl. She naps during the days. Or walks over to El Rio after school to hang out with some of the girls there. And then late at night I see her flipping through her AP English book. Mumbling to herself and making notes.

And Mama reads too. The newspaper. Articles on her laptop

computer. Sometimes she stays in bed past noon lost in a TV show or book. And I wonder if this is what she did when she was a girl. If after being in the spotlight. On the radio. And practicing for five hours a day. She retreated to her room to be alone. I wonder what lessons she learned while traveling. What her parents made her do to keep up with her studies. What it must have been like to be so talented and so young.

QUESTIONS I HAVE FOR BLACK GIRLS LIKE ME

posted April 25th

Dear K

I love the title. LOL. You know I always have questions. And that tagline is perfect. I am so glad you figured out the password. I knew you would.

I've been thinking about that word Katy called you. A lot. I never got to tell you about my trip to the Museum of African American History and Culture. It was super awkward to walk through some of the exhibits with my mom. When we arrived. We took a big elevator to the very bottom floor of the museum. When we got out we were in a dark cramped gallery with pictures and artifacts from the slave trade. It felt like we were IN a slave ship. The rooms were narrow and triangular. It was hot and crowded and dark. My mom kept gasping at all the images of black people in chains. And she was holding my hand really tight. I dunno. I felt like. She was making a big scene. And that everyone was looking at me. Like maybe she never really thought about how bad it must have been. But I have.

When I was standing in that crowded space with her. I felt alone. And then later in the cafeteria for lunch my mom said:

"I'm so glad we've come so far as a country." But have we? Not if people are still using the N-word. I guess what I am trying to say is that the museum made me feel both small and proud. Like. Look at all the great things black people have done even though we went through—and still go through—so much.

I do know that I feel most powerful when I'm on the balance beam. When I land all my jumps and stick my landing. That's when I feel the strongest. Like I can do anything.

Your BFF

L

PS Here is a picture I took of a Billie Holiday "master disc." You're welcome. ☺

Homeschool Group

Almost two weeks after pulling us out of school Mama announces that we'll be joining a homeschool group.

"It took me forever to find a group that's not überreligious but the founder of the group is a political science professor at the University of New Mexico named Mr. John. So the group is pretty liberal." She tells us.

"Are there any high schoolers?" Eve asks.

"There are a couple of 8th graders who are doing high school level work. So. You'll be in good company. And Makeda. There are plenty of kids your age in the group as well."

"Great!" Eve yells. "Eighth graders. So basically I'll be babysitting. This is going to be so fun."

Mama ignores her and turns to me. "Any questions from you Makeda? You're very quiet these days."

So are you. I want to say. But instead I ask: "Are there any black kids in the group?"

"Well I don't see why color has to matter so much. But I think there is a set of twin girls who are Chinese American. Mr. John assured me it was a very diverse group in other ways.

And Mr. John's son Huck is mixed. His mother is from Peru originally. I think you'll like the other kids. If you give them a chance."

I bite my tongue. I think about Lena. I miss her. But I do need some friends here too. Maybe Mama is right. It will be nice to have company since Eve doesn't really like to play anymore and except for Lena and our blog there's hardly anyone to talk to these days.

"Alright then." Mama continues. "You're going to have to give it a chance because I've volunteered us to host the group at our place this week. So. We need to get the house ready. Now."

We Spend the Next Two Days Cleaning

Our rooms. The kitchen. The bathrooms. Mama even makes us comb the yard for trash. On Thursday morning we grab pillows from all over the house and arrange them in a circle on the floor of the sunroom. At 9am the group starts to arrive. I watch from the front window as cars pull slowly into our long driveway and let kids out. Mama and Eve greet everyone at the door and then I usher people to the sunroom. Mr. John is the last to arrive with his son. And when we all sit down the sunroom is filled with about ten of us. I look around. No one speaks. It is so quiet. As if they hardly know each other. *What kind of group is this?*

"Good morning everyone!" Mr. John starts. "Let's go around and introduce ourselves. Everyone say your name and one thing that you think makes you unique."

Carl and his little sister Emma are up first. They are dedicated Christians but "We accept all of god's people. No matter your faith or beliefs." Carl says for the both of them.

Melody is next. She is frail. With vampire pale skin. Short brown hair and round glasses. She looks at her hands and tells us she's obsessed with Pokémon Go and loves drawing.

Vienna and her two younger twin sisters Amy and Alyse follow. "I'm a dancer." Vienna starts. She's sitting a little outside of the circle stretching her long legs. "I dance ballet and modern with the New Mexico Youth Company. I'm planning to go to Juilliard by the time I'm sixteen. (I'm thirteen now.)" The twins sit next to her. They wear coordinated teal and purple floral rompers but Alyse has a short bob haircut and Amy wears a long ponytail.

"I'm in 3rd grade." Amy starts. "And I think eating meat is murder. I'm going to be a veterinarian."

"And I'm Alyse. I think bacon is delicious. I'm going to be a five-star chef."

Then there is Huck. Mr. John's son. Huck is in 7th grade but looks like he could be in high school. He has brown eyes and shaggy black hair that falls over his eyes. "My parents named me after the book *The Adventures of Huckleberry Finn*. I love maps. I got fifth place in the National Geography Bee last year. This year I'm hoping to place in the top three." He tells the group. His voice is calming. Soft. Like snow hitting the mountains.

After Huck a small boy named Jesse introduces himself. But I don't hear anything he says. I'm still thinking about Huck's voice. I want to know where he's traveled. What his favorite word is. His favorite country. *Does he look at maps the way I do?* I wonder.

Eve's voice snaps me out of my daydream. She's sitting next

to me in the circle. "I'm Eve. but I guess you guys know that already since I met most of you on your way in. I'm in 9th grade. I like to act."

And then it is my turn. All eyes focus on me. Even Huck's. And I feel my face get warm. "Makeda. But my friends call me Keda. I'm in 6th grade. I love jazz music. I wish I could sing like Billie Holiday."

"Who's he?" Melody asks.

"No—" I start to say but before I can finish Huck jumps in.

"Billie Holiday is a SHE. And a very famous blues and jazz singer from the 1940s. I saw a play about her in New York last summer."

"Yes." Mr. John chimes in. "We can listen to some of her songs later. But now it's time to move on. Thanks for sharing everyone."

After introductions Mr. John starts the lesson of the day. The group has been learning about the Civil Rights Movement. About Martin Luther King Jr. and Malcolm X. About segregation in the South. Lunch counter sit-ins. Bus boycotts and marches. I've been reading all about the Civil Rights Movement in my book. In fact I've been writing and illustrating a whole magazine about the Little Rock Nine Emmett Till Martin Luther King Jr. and so on. I look around the room at the other kids who seem to be in awe or shock or disbelief. *Don't they know their American history?*

"Dumping boiling coffee on people is not a very Christian thing to do." Carl can't contain himself any longer.

"Yeah." Emma chimes in. "Couldn't they just let the colored people eat at the lunch counter?"

"I think you mean African American." Mr. John corrects her. "We don't call them colored anymore. It's just not correct."

I hope nobody can tell that my ears are prickling hot. I can't help it. I look around the room at all the eager faces. I feel like throwing up. I just want to yell I AM THEM even though I'm worried they don't see me that way.

And then I catch Huck's eyes. He smiles. And just like that. I soften. Huck looks at me as if we already know one another. Like he is studying my face. Memorizing it for later.

Tangled

Mama means to be gentle but she's ripping apart my locs just like she pulls up weeds in the backyard: rough and fast. Ever since I can remember it's been this way. Mama with her YouTube tutorials and tubs full of different creams conditioners oils hair ties pins hooks and headbands all meant for taming natural hair. And me sitting on the floor in front of her trying not to cry.

"Makeda. Sit still. You're squirming too much. I know I can get this right."

But I can't stop squirming today. We are in the sunroom. It's late morning. I am tender-headed. Always have been. And any little pull or snag sends a sharp pain down my neck and into my back.

But ever since I was called the N-word. I've been tearing out the locs at the back of my neck. It hurts but I can't stop. And until Mama starts making her way across my scalp today. Separating the locs that have grown together and twisting my new growth. I don't realize how bad it's gotten. Not until I hear Mama gasp.

"What have you done?!" She asks shoving my head forward

and running her fingers along the back of my patchy head. "You've made a mess of your beautiful hair."

"I dunno." I say biting my lip.

We are silent. Mama covers her hands with grease and rubs it as best she can into my baby hairs and patchiness. Her hands feel like spiders. Crawling all over me.

"Stop!" I say. Scooting away from her hands. "I don't want to do this anymore. I want it off."

"We can take a break."

"No. I just don't want this anymore." I say. Lifting my uneven locs up. I feel tears pooling in my eyes. *Don't cry don't cry don't cry.* How do I tell Mama that what I really don't want is her hands in my hair. It always hurts. She tries but it hurts. The whole reason I have locs in the first place is because she told me it was the easiest way to keep my hair nice. "Low maintenance." She'd said. So she started my hair in locs when I was seven. And I've worn it that way ever since.

But when Eve was younger and before I had locs Mama used to do our hair on the same day. I'd watch Mama brush Eve's thick straight hair so easily. Then watch her create two perfectly even tight French braids identical to hers before sending Eve off on her way. When it was my turn Mama would pull and fight and try to braid my curly hair the same way but it never came out as smooth as Eve's. It was always uneven. Bits of hairs escaped and stuck out in odd places. And sometimes. When she was really frustrated. Mama would mutter: "I just don't understand why it has to be so difficult." And it always felt like she was talking about me. *I am difficult.*

"Oh. I see." Mama is quiet now. "Well." She says after a long pause. "You're old enough to decide what you want."

"I want something new. A change. And I want to go to a black hair salon. Like the one Lena gets to go to every week." I say before I can stop myself.

To my surprise Mama doesn't protest even though she looks like she might cry. "Ok." She says. "But let's see if we can find a natural hair salon. I won't have you burning your hair off with chemicals like Lena."

An hour later we jump in the van. We drive across town and pull up in front of a low building with a hot pink window decal that reads STORMY'S NATURAL HAIR & LOCS. Through the glass windows I see at least three black women sitting in chairs. Talking and reading magazines.

"Maybe they don't have time for me?" I say. All of a sudden not sure I belong here with my patchy hair and ashy elbows. And my white mama.

"Nonsense." Mama says getting out of the car. "I called. They said they had room for you today."

We walk inside and the bells on the door tinkle. All eyes

turn to us and conversation stops. A black woman with the most beautiful locs I've ever seen walks over. They are thin and dyed a burgundy red with different gold beads in them. They hang regal and neat down past her shoulders. She looks like an actual queen. A goddess. I bite my tongue to keep from gasping.

"Can I help you?" She says. Looking at me with a small smile that disappears when she meets eyes with Mama.

"Yes. Uh. We're looking for Stormy. I called ahead about my daughter?"

"Your daughter?" Stormy startles looking down at me again. This time with a softer smile. "Oh yes. Your daughter. Well I'm Stormy. Welcome to my shop. What's your name baby girl?" She says putting her arm around my shoulders and leading me to her chair in front of the mirrors.

"This is Makeda." Mama answers. Following behind us.

"Hi." I squeak as I settle into the worn black leather chair that smells like cocoa butter and sweat. "Keda. I'm Keda."

"Ok well now Keda. What can I do for you?" Stormy is already running her hands through my hair. She pulls my messy locs up into a thick bunch and clucks her tongue when she sees the patchy area at the back of my head. In the mirrors. I see Stormy catch eyes with one of the other women in the salon who raises her eyebrow as if to say: *What on earth?!* I feel my body heating from within. My ears hot hot hot.

"I want a buzz cut." I say. When I find my words again. But they are the wrong words.

"A what?" Stormy laughs a little and then stops herself. "Baby girl. You mean you want me to give you the chop? You want me to cut off all this length you been working on?"

"Um. Yeah. The chop. I want the chop. I want short hair. Something I can do myself."

Stormy shakes her head. And looks at Mama who is standing so close to me I can feel her breath on my right ear. "And this is ok with you?"

"It's her choice." Mama says. Looking slightly defeated. "I told her as long as it's a natural style and as long as she can use natural products it's fine by me. I won't have her burning her hair straight like some black women. It's just so sad. Natural hair is so beautiful. Why try to conform to some white ideal of beauty? And your locs are so lovely. You must understand—"

"Well that's not really how it works." Stormy cuts Mama off midsentence. "We don't 'burn our hair off.'" Then I watch Stormy take a sharp breath to stop herself from saying more. She points Mama across the room. "Why don't you have a seat over there in our waiting area. I'll take it from here."

Mama's cheeks flare. But she goes quiet and slides into a chair across the room. When she's out of earshot Stormy comes around the front of the chair and leans over to look into my eyes.

"Ok then." Stormy continues. "How short do you want it? You want a tapered cut? A TWA? A fade into mohawk? A faux-hawk? A twistout? Do you want to be able to finger-curl it into a short look? Tell me. I got you."

As she lists off style after style my tongue goes numb. I had no idea there were so many options.

"I just know I don't want locs anymore." I manage.

Stormy smiles and shakes her head. "Ok baby girl. Let's look at some pictures. Maybe that will help."

After we scroll through some pictures of black actresses on Stormy's iPad I decide on a TWA—a "Teeny Weeny Afro." Kinda like Lupita Nyong'o!

"Good choice." Stormy assures me. "You won't even be able to tell about this." She says motioning to the patches where I pulled my locs out. "I'll give you a little fade in the back so it looks like it's supposed to be this way but we'll blend it up on the side so you can still have some length."

I close my eyes as my locs fall onto the floor around me like fallen tree branches. I feel the weight come off and sigh with relief. After "the chop" Stormy leads me to the sinks. Then she massages my newly shorn head with peppermint shampoo until it tingles like Christmas. Before I leave Stormy gives me a bag full of natural products to use on my new hair and skin. Some she makes on her own at the shop.

"You come back now." She calls as we head out. "In about two weeks. And I'll even you out. Make sure to keep it conditioned too." And I know she's talking to me.

On the way home I can't stop looking at my TWA in the mirror. I'm not bald. But my curls are tight and close to my scalp with a little more length on the top than on the side and in the back. The back is smooth and even when I run my hand over it.

"Very chic." Mama says. "I think I like it. It will just take some getting used to."

"Thanks." I say. Beaming.

"You kinda look like a little boy." Eve says when she sees my hair later that evening.

"She looks like an African princess!" Mama corrects sharply. "Why don't we pick you out some pretty earrings at the mall this week?"

But I don't care if I look like a boy or an African princess. I don't care about the mall or earrings either. "Just leave me alone." I say to Eve as I head to my room. And when I get there I look at myself in the closet mirrors and say: *This is me.*

Later that night I get on the computer and upload a picture of my new hair. Then I type a post:

posted May 12th

QUESTIONS I HAVE FOR BLACK GIRLS (WITH HAIR) LIKE ME

Who decides what kind of hair is beautiful?

Do you ever just want to tell your mom: "White lady stop! You don't know what you're doing!"

Do you remember the first black woman to ever wash your hair?

What did it feel like? Did it hurt?

Or did it feel like home?

Huckleberry Finn

It's been a little over one week since I cut my locs off and I love the way it feels. Every day I condition it and watch my little curls tighten and gleam. Mama never takes me to the mall to get earrings but that's ok. I am still happy she let me cut it. I have plenty of earrings already and mostly I just like to wear my thin gold hoops. Lena's only comment on the picture I uploaded is "QUEENLY." So I think she likes it too. She hasn't had much time for our blog this week.

But today. I take extra care with my hair. My outfit. Homeschool group is at Mr. John's house and that means Huck will be there. I look in the mirror now and wonder what the others will think.

"It's time to go girls!" Papa yells from the living room. He's dropping us off before rehearsal and Mama will pick us up this afternoon. She's still sleeping from what I can tell even though it's almost ten. I take one more look in the mirror. I'm wearing jeans and a polka dot black and white shirt with ruffle sleeves. "Very chic." I say before grabbing my jean jacket and running out the door.

Huck's house is also in the valley. About a ten-minute drive from ours. Instead of a lawn full of patchy grass the front yard is full of gravel paths big rocks and cactus. It's also a one-story house but it's made of white bricks instead of adobe.

"Ok scoops." Papa says as we pull up to the curb. "Mama will get you at four. Have fun!"

Eve slams her door and heads inside. I give Papa a kiss on the cheek. "Bye."

"You look great!" He says squeezing my hand. "They're gonna love your hair."

I feel my cheeks flare with heat and then stick out my tongue.

Papa grins and drives off.

When I get inside Mr. John is the only one there. "Hey Makeda! Look at you. New hair?"

"Yeah." I say. "Where is everyone?"

"Out back. I thought we'd start with some games today. Everyone is full of energy. Go ahead. I'll see you out there."

I drop my bag in the hallway. I smooth my shirt and head out back. Everyone is there. Vienna and Eve are whispering by a lawn chair. But the rest of the group is standing on a concrete patio playing four square.

Before I can say "hi" Jesse sees me and screams: "WHOA. KEDA. WHAT HAPPENED TO YOUR HAIR?"

Alyse who has the ball drops it as everyone turns to look at me. My cheeks explode with heat. But instead of sticking out my tongue I hear myself say: “WHAT HAPPENED TO YOUR FACE JESSE?!”

“Oh snap!” Amy says.

“She trolled you for sure.” Vienna says coming up beside me. “She got it cut. So what? It’s her hair.”

“It just looks so . . . short.” Jesse tries to recover.

“Guys. Come on! Let’s keep playing.” Huck’s voice cuts Jesse off. “It’s just hair. I think it looks nice. Now can we please play?”

With that Alyse calls out the category “COLORS” and throws the ball back into play. I stand in line waiting for my turn but my heart is pounding. *I think it looks nice.* Did he really say that?

“Keda! You’re in.” Melody yells. And then I am in the game. Across from Huck who has the ball. He calls out the category “COUNTRIES IN CENTRAL AMERICA” and hits the ball into my square. “COSTA RICA.” I yell and slam it back into his. “PANAMA.” He yells and then hits it to his right into Carl’s square. “BRAZIL!” Carl screams and then slams it into my square.

“You’re out!” I say. The ball rolling out of my square into the yard.

“No I’m not!”

"Yeah. You are. Brazil is not in Central America. It's in South America."

"Yes it is!" Carl insists.

"Dude. Keda's right. You're out." Huck says running back to the game with the ball. "Come on. Let's keep going." And when he hands me back the ball. Our fingers touch for a second. And I tingle all over.

And later that night. After four square. After our lesson for the day. After Huck gives us all a tour of his room which looks like the inside of a pirate ship. After Mama comes to get us. After dinner. After I take a shower and wash and condition my own hair. My new curls glisten. I stand in my room with all the windows open. I pull out the shea butter Stormy gave me. I lotion my neck. My shoulders. My elbows. My knees. Toes. I stand in front of the mirror and imagine my body as a continent. A map. I study this new map of my body. And I hum and hum with delight.

Hot Springs

On Memorial Day weekend Papa gets three days off of work just to spend with us. No rehearsals. No chamber recording sessions. Not one business meeting in preparation for the symphony's upcoming international summer tour.

"Just me and my girls!" He tells us at dinner on Friday night.

"I'm a woman. Not a girl." Mama corrects him.

"Right right. Just me and my girls and my woman!" He says with a wink.

"That's worse! Daniel. You know I hate being called a woman like that. It's so possessive. You don't own me."

"What about 'just me and my fine females'?" Eve says. Winking back at Papa.

"Or. 'Me and my smokin' ladies'?" I say. And I watch as Mama finally cracks a smile.

"Very funny." She says. "Let's just all be sexist pigs."

Early Saturday morning we pack up some food and hike to the hot springs in the Santa Fe National Forest. It's a three-mile hike through the winding paths but the trees cover us with shade so it's not too hot. Still. Mama makes us all wear dorky straw hats so we don't burn our skin. As soon as we start walking Eve and I push them back so they hang around our necks by the drawstrings. Mama and Papa are ahead of us. Not only is Mama wearing a big straw hat but she is covered head to toe in a flowy white long sleeve shirt and pants that are supposed to protect her from the sun.

"Mama looks like a beekeeper in that outfit." Eve whispers.

"I know. Or like she's going on a safari." I giggle.

"Or like Colonel Sanders from KFC."

We both laugh hard. Mama and Papa stop to consult the map. And Eve and I grab handfuls of dried fruit and nuts from the snack bag to keep our energy up. We've never been to a hot spring before. But Mama and Papa promise us it will be worth it.

"New Mexico has some of the finest hot springs in the whole world." Papa says. We are about a mile away and resting by a large boulder. Mama passes around the water bottle and we all take big gulps from it.

"Is it like a hot tub?" I ask.

"Sort of." Mama pants. Catching her breath. "It's a natural pool of hot water that develops because of volcanic or geothermal heat in the earth below."

"Wait. Did you say volcanic?! Is this even safe?" Eve is paying attention now.

"Yes. It's perfectly safe. Don't worry. You'll see. But we

should keep moving. We've only got a little bit left to go." Papa picks up a stick from the path and waves it over his head. "This is the perfect walking stick!" He yells and then forges ahead stabbing it into the ground next to him as he powers on.

"What is it with men and big sticks?" Mama jokes with us. "Just ignore him. I'll bet he loses the stick by the end of today."

We laugh and follow Papa up the path. Mama's face is red with effort but glowing all the same and it feels nice to be doing something together. To be laughing and joking and moving our bodies. When we get close the air begins to smell like pennies or metal or rotten eggs. Mama tells us it's the sulfur and that it's normal for the hot springs to smell this way. I am expecting a round pool with concrete all around it like in a hotel but when we arrive the pools are shallow and spread out and all different shapes and sizes. One looks like a kidney bean. The other a small triangle under a rock. Another a long rectangular pool under a cove of trees.

"Looks like we're the first ones here today!" Papa is delighted. "Let's get in!"

We find a picnic table and drop our things. We strip down to our bathing suits and even though it is still mostly shady Mama makes us slather our skin with sunscreen and then wait ten minutes for it to dry. "Always protect your skin! The sun causes cancer." She lectures.

I roll my eyes. The thick SPF 50 sunscreen she makes us both use is too thick. By the time I have it all over me I look like a zombie and it never really sinks into my dark skin. And when I get it wet it's even worse. I look like an actual ash monster.

"Anna." Papa yells from the kidney-shaped pool. "Come on! The water is delightful."

Mama steps cautiously over rocks and pine needles and joins him.

"Let's try that one." Eve says pointing to a smaller pool. Hidden partially behind a big rock.

"Sure."

We step our way over to it. Drop our towels and I back quickly into the water. The spring bubbles and steams. And it really is almost as hot as a hot tub. I close my eyes and take a deep breath with my mouth to avoid the smell. But before I open them Eve screams. "Keda! Get out get out get out. Ewwwww! Get out."

"What's wrong!"

"Behind you! Get out."

I turn around and see a naked man. Partially hidden by the shadow of the rock. A man with long stringy hair and a peace tattoo right above his you-know-what. Sitting. In the spring.

"Good morning!" He says. "No need to get out. There's room. It's a beautiful day for the springs."

"Um no thanks." I jump out so fast I forget my towel.

Eve screams. And I scream. And we run back to our clothes and start putting them on as fast as we can.

"What on earth is wrong?" Papa yells from the kidney pool.

But at that moment the peace tattoo man walks up and waves. He's still naked. "Good morning! I think I scared your girls. Most people don't realize that clothing is optional here."

And that puts an end to our adventure. Mama leaps out and joins us. Pulling on her clothes. And Papa sits frozen in the pool with a sheepish look on his face until Mama yells at him to get out. We hike down that mountain so fast. And it's not till we're on the road home that Eve says: "Why on earth would you tattoo a peace sign above your penis?" And then we all laugh so hard we cry.

Moonlight Sonata

When Papa is home. Like tonight. Eve and I give recitals in the living room. After our hike I sit at the piano and look at the sheet music while Mama Eve and Papa sit on the couch in front of me. I always play first because if I play second Eve's song gets all mixed up with my song and I forget the notes altogether. There is nothing worse than hearing Papa's frustrated sighs as I try to recover by picking and testing different keys with my fingers. "Just read the music." He'll nudge. "The music is right in front of you." But that's the thing. Notes on the page look like some foreign alphabet to me. Instead of reading them I like to close my eyes and imagine the song as a movie or a shape or sometimes a dance. This helps me and my hands shimmy over the keys as if they've known the steps all along.

Tonight I am playing the *Moonlight Sonata*. Eve will play *Für Elise*. Papa leaves at the end of the week for his international tour with the symphony. He'll be gone all of June July and some of August and it really will be "just us girls." I've been practicing for weeks to learn the whole piece perfectly. Every Wednesday morning Mrs. Umanski has been drilling us on scales arpeggios and music theory before letting us practice our new pieces. I pay extra attention to the notes at my lesson as well. If Mrs. Umanski suspects I'm playing the song by ear she raps my knuckles lightly while barking: "Start over and this time keep your eyes up!"

But the *Moonlight Sonata* is my favorite. I know the notes by heart now. I've been waiting weeks for this. To feel Papa nodding his head in rhythm with me and only me. I close my eyes and get into position. The keys feel like the cool marble of a museum floor. Then softly. With eyes still closed. I start. The whole room swells. And I do not open my eyes. Not once. My fingers fly. Just fly. Mimicking each note perfectly like little brown thrashers gossiping in the trees.

Insomnia (noun)

The inability to sleep.

It is around 1am. The Georgia Belles are nowhere to be found and my room is thick with darkness. I am in my bed. Sweaty from changing positions over and over again. Trying to get comfortable enough to dream. Outside in the distance I hear wild dogs crying. Their howls low and full of lonely. I am still not used to these desert sounds. To the way the front yard outside my window looks bare and still in the moonlight. How the ground seems to crawl with shadows. How the mountains shape-shift against the sky. Mama and Papa stopped arguing hours ago. But I can still hear pieces of their conversation echoing around in my head.

It's good you're leaving. I need some space. The girls and I will be just fine.

Are you going to punish me forever Anna? I'm trying to provide for you and the girls. This is the job. You knew what it required.

I know. I know. But I'd like to provide too Daniel. I didn't sign up for this. I was a star!

Then why don't you start up your teaching practice again? Get some students. I can help you make some connections—

I don't want your help!

Then what do you want? You sulk around all day. You haven't picked up your violin in months. What kind of example is that for the girls?

I do EVERYTHING around here. I was the one who packed up all of our stuff remember? Who drove three days straight to get us here. You come home and marvel at how the house is coming together. Who do you think does that? Who is taking the girls to piano lessons to the library? Who is making sure they are safe and getting an education?

Anna. You didn't even consult me. You just pulled them out of school. I know we've talked about homeschooling the girls. But do you really think you can handle this right now? It's almost summer so for now keeping them out of school is fine. But I'm not sure we should next fall.

Absolutely not. They will not go back to that oppressive school. And how dare you question my ability to educate them! I'm self-taught you know. I read more books in a month than you do all year.

I'm not questioning your intelligence. I'm just worried that you are not at your best. That you need to take some time to get healthy. Maybe talk to someone again. A professional.

No. Daniel. We. We are not at our best. Don't pretend like you're not a part of this equation. And I don't need a therapist. It never works for me. You know that. I'm just fine. I'm not going to have another nervous breakdown. That was years ago. I've kept it together haven't I? Just go on your tour. You've barely been here anyway.

At some point I pressed each end of the pillow so close to my ears that all I could hear were their muffled voices. And now. Hours later. The house is quiet. Too quiet. I sneak out of bed and down the hallway. I see Papa's bags waiting by the front door. His shuttle will be here in a few hours. I hear a rustle in the sunroom behind me. Papa is sitting there. Meditating.

"Can't sleep?" He asks me. His eyes still closed.

I shake my head.

"Did we keep you up?"

"Sort of." I say taking a seat next to him on his yoga mat.

"I'm sorry if we scared you. Your mom and I. Well. We love each other a lot. But we're two very passionate people. We fight. But we always snap back eventually. You don't need to worry about us. We love you very much. It's not about you. I hope you know that."

I don't know. It sure feels like we are the problem sometimes. If Mama had never had Eve or adopted me she might still be playing with symphonies all over the world. She might be happier. But I don't say this. Instead I ask: "How does it work?"

"Meditating?"

"Yeah."

"Well. I try to relax my body. Take deep breaths in and out. In and out. The goal is to not think. To just focus on your breath."

"I don't think I can stop thinking."

"That's ok. It takes time."

We sit together then. Just breathing. In and out. In and out. But I can't clear my mind.

"Papa?"

"Little scoop?"

"I'm tired. Will you come sit in my room?"

"Sure. But just for a little bit."

Papa grabs his mat and we tiptoe back to my room. Papa tucks me in like he used to when I was smaller. All the blankets tight around my body so that I am snug.

"You know we're going to FaceTime while I'm gone. And I'll be back before you know it."

I nod.

"Take care of your mama ok? I don't like leaving for so long. But I'll be back before you know it."

"We'll be ok." I say.

Papa smiles and kisses me on the cheek. Then he sits down in the middle of my floor and starts to meditate again. I know I shouldn't be scared. But I am. *Don't leave.* I say in my head. *Don't leave don't leave don't leave me.* I listen to him breathing in and out in and out. Eventually I slip away into a light sleep. When I wake up Papa is gone. And so are his bags.

Part II: SUMMER

June in the Desert

Is dull. Dry. Full of coiled bull snakes and crumbling mud. Even the chickens have started to lose their golden fluff. Turned over time into dirty coats of brown and red feathers. And Mama too has lost interest in our routine. Three days after Papa leaves she looks up from the book she is reading at the table. Her hair wild and unwashed.

"Where's your sister?" She says.

"Working."

"Working where?"

"At the ice cream shop. She told you and Papa last week. She got a job at the Melody Icey down the street? Remember?"

"Huh. Good for her. What about you?"

"What do you mean?"

"What are you going to do today?"

"Dunno." I say.

"Better figure it out soon. I'd start with a book." Then she goes back to reading.

It is Monday. Midday. Mama and I are still in our pjs. The heat of the afternoon starting to simmer and sting. Or maybe it is my dry skin. I've run out of Stormy's shea butter and no matter how many bottles of the organic unscented lotion I use I can never seem to get rid of the ash. Day after day I slather on layer after layer. Watching the thin liquid sink into my skin in seconds. The sun beating down on me until it's gone.

Whenever Mama and I go to the grocery store. I sneak away to the beauty aisle. I open the Jergens bottles. Let the smell of processed cocoa butter smack me in the face. I dream about my birth mom. Imagine her in a room with lavender walls. A dresser filled with pretty bottles of scented things and oils for my hair. In this daydream we never speak. Or touch. I sit next to her on the bed. She smiles. And then we rub our bodies with thick lotion until we sparkle. Until our skin is golden-black. Until the moon dresses us with the shimmer we deserve. I want a mother who shines like that. Who is as beautiful as wet sea stone at midnight. But I only have the Georgia Belles guiding me. Their humming and chattering around my room at night.

I want a mother who sees me. Glistening. Even under all this cracked and flaking skin.

Sweet Tomato

"I signed you up for Girl Scouts." Mama announces to me a week later. The three of us are at Sweet Tomato. A local restaurant that Mama likes because they serve all natural meat and organic produce. Eve and I pick at our pieces of dry artichoke and spinach pizza on whole wheat crust. "It's much better than Domino's isn't it?" Mama says to us.

"Not really." Eve says under her breath catching my eye. I give her a small smile. But we don't say anything else because this is the first time we've been out all together since Papa left ten days ago.

"Makeda you start tomorrow. The troop meets at the community center. I can drive you or you can bike. It's only a mile away."

"I don't want to go. I'm too old to start now."

"Nonsense. You've always wanted to be a Girl Scout. You used to beg me in Baltimore. You wanted to join Lena's troop remember?"

"That was three years ago." I mumble but Mama is not listening.

"You've just been hanging around the house." She continues. "Your sister has a job. I thought you'd like to be around some girls your age. Why don't you just try it? I just . . ."

And then for no reason at all Mama starts crying. Right there at the table over a stupid Girl Scouts troop. "I just want to give you girls everything. I want you to be happy."

I know Mama loves me. I just wonder if she likes me. If she likes any of us. Her family. Some days I feel like I am in her way. And others like she can't live without me. One moment she is telling me to get out of her face. Read a book. Be independent. And the next she is begging me to come snuggle with her. To brush her long hair or bring her some tea. I do it all. I try to figure out what she needs before she needs it. But then she'll yell at me to stop hovering or she'll start crying over what feels like nothing. It's confusing.

Eve and I look at each other now as Mama blows her nose into a napkin. Eve raises her eyebrow and I shake my head so she raises it higher as if to say: *Just do it.*

"Fine." I say. "You don't have to cry. I'll bike there. But I'm not wearing that ugly green vest."

"Oh Makeda. Give it a chance. I think you'll love it." Mama sighs smiling through her sniffles.

"And Girl Scout cookies are SOOOO good!" Eve chimes in. "You can sell them to me Keda. I'll buy them."

"Sure." I say. But I can't even think about cookies. I have a bad feeling in my gut. How can I tell Mama that I'm worried about leaving her at home? All by herself.

My Bike

Used to be Mama's old bike from when she was a kid. It's dark purple like an eggplant with a banana seat and pink and yellow tassels on the handlebars. Eve tells me that it's "vintage" that it's so old it's back in style again. The next afternoon I take it out of the garage and ride it to Girl Scouts.

I love riding my bike. I pump my legs hard so that I am going as fast as I can. I stand up on the pedals and just cruise. I let the wind whip my face and it feels like I am flying. Like instead of being stuck between two mothers. Stuck in the desert. Stuck without my best friend. Without a papa. I am free again. To take myself wherever the road leads me.

The ride to Girl Scouts is too short. Soon I am hopping off and locking my bike out front.

"Are you the new girl?" I hear a voice behind me say. "I'm Lydia. My mom's the troop leader. She sent me out here to meet you. I'm going to be your buddy for the day."

Lydia is wearing cat-eye purple glasses and a shift dress with multicolor flowers all over it. Her green vest clashes with the bright orange petals but she wears it proudly. She has about a million pins and patches she's earned. They look heavy hanging off of her vest.

"Yeah." I say. Gathering my things. "I'm Keda."

"That's a pretty name." Lydia says then. "Well. Do you want to go in? And meet everyone?"

"Sure."

"Cool bike by the way." Lydia says.

I grin. Maybe this won't be so bad after all.

"Lydia you lie. That bike is crazy looking." A girl who has just been dropped off says to us now. She's a little taller than us both and has sharp brown eyes and long black hair pulled up into a high ponytail. As she walks toward us her ponytail swishes from side to side like a lullaby. She's beautiful.

"Hey Alma." Lydia says. Her voice turned quiet and shaky. "This. This is Keda. She's new."

Alma looks me up and down. Her glossed lips pull at the corners into a fake smile. "Hey." She says. "No offense new girl. But that's a hipster-ass bike. Like for real. Where did you even find that?"

"It was my mom's." I say. "It's vintage."

"*It was my mom's. It's vintage.*" Alma says. Mocking my voice. "You need to loosen up. You sound like a robot."

"Alma." Lydia tries to break in. But Alma pays no attention.

"Anyways. Welcome to the troop or whatever. I'll see you inside new girl. You got a lot to catch up on."

"My name's Keda." I say after her.

Alma lifts up her right arm and waves it. "Sure. Ok." She says disappearing into the front doors of the center.

"She gets nicer." Lydia says apologetically. But I get the feeling Lydia is scared of her too.

And even though Lydia is my buddy for the rest of the day. Even though our troop leader Mrs. Karen makes all the girls introduce themselves. I soon learn who is in charge. Alma. She swishes her ponytail and talks over everyone and all the girls follow her around like she is royalty. And every time I talk Alma looks at me like I'm an alien. Like she's trying to figure out what planet I came from.

Happy Birthday America

On July 4th Mama wakes up bursting with energy. Or maybe she's never even gone to bed. She runs around the living room unpacking her sheet music and violin scores. Sorting and resorting them into messy piles on the floor. Eve has the day off (finally!) and Mama promised we could all drive to see the fireworks downtown later. Eve and I tiptoe around the kitchen now trying not to make a noise or ask Mama if she needs help. We eat our oatmeal in the sunroom with the door closed.

"Want to watch music videos on my phone?" Eve offers scooping the last bite into her mouth.

"Sure." I scoot closer to her. So that our shoulders are touching.

"It's all clear to me now! I need everything organized so I can start fresh. A new beginning." We hear Mama talking to herself from the next room.

Eve turns the volume up all the way on her phone. "You pick first."

I type in Nina Simone "Feeling Good" and even though it's

not a real video but just a recording with pictures of Nina Eve lets me watch the whole thing.

"I like that song." She says when it's done. "Now my turn." And Eve picks the song "Roxie" from the musical *Chicago*. She knows all the words and so do I since we saw it live in New York two years ago on a family vacation. When the song ends I grab the phone from Eve and type something in secretly.

"Remember this?" I say jumping up and getting into position. I stand in front of Eve with my palms pressed together in prayer.

"'How Do You Solve a Problem Like Maria'!" Eve laughs. And then she gets up and stands next to me in the same pose. *The Sound of Music* is another one of our favorites. We watch it whenever we can. When the song starts we take turns singing and pretending we are the nuns. We shake our heads and act very concerned about all the mischief that Maria is causing in the abbey.

"Let's keep it going." Eve laughs when the song ends and types in "My Favorite Things."

We yell-sing. Dancing around in our pjs just like the Von Trapp kids.

Midsong Mama flings the door to the sunroom open. "Girls!" She yells. "Have you seen the paper shredder?"

We shake our heads and I feel Eve moving closer to me. "Mama." Eve says slowly. "What do you need it for?"

"Oh I think it's in the garage! Yes. Yes. That's where I've seen it." With that Mama flurries out and runs into the garage.

"Let's do another song!" I turn back to Eve with a smile but her face is a hard stone.

She wrinkles her nose and bites her lip. "Follow me." She says after a beat.

We tiptoe back out to the living room. Mama has dragged the paper shredder into the middle of the floor and plugged it in. She's wearing her nightgown and nothing else. Her large breasts swing slightly from side to side as she begins to shred every single piece of her music. Sheet by sheet. "I just need to start over." Mama mumbles to herself over and over again. "A fresh start."

"Should we stop her?" I ask.

"No." Eve says her hands on her hips. "Come with me."

I follow Eve again. This time we duck into the laundry room across from Mama and Papa's room.

"Listen." Eve says in her annoying big sister voice. "We might not make it to fireworks tonight. And I need you to not complain about it ok?"

"What! But Mama promised." I can't help but whine.

"I know. It sucks. But listen. We just need to let Mama do whatever she's doing ok? Stay out of her way."

"Ok." I gulp. But my head feels like it might explode. I stay out of Mama's way all the time. "But why?" I can't help saying out loud. "Why can't she just be fine so we can see fireworks like a normal family? Nobody keeps their promises these days. It's not fair!"

Eve's brow unfurrows. Her shoulders slump. But she doesn't yell at me. She just shrugs her shoulders and bites her lip as if to say: *I'm sorry.*

"Want to get out of here?" Eve says after I calm down. Her voice soft like it used to be when she let me hang out in her room more. "We can take a walk to the bird farm?"

I do. Want to get out. But for some reason I also want to yell and scream and throw myself onto the hallway floor like I am a toddler. I hold back my tears. "Sure." I say.

We try to tell Mama where we are going. But she just waves her hand at us and continues shredding. So we leave through the back gate and walk along the ditch behind our house into the droning light of the morning. Eve charges ahead.

"Stop walking so fast." I yell at her.

"Walk faster chicken legs!" She yells back with a grin.

I stick out my tongue and try to keep up. I'm glad to be out of the house. Even if it means walking in Eve's dust.

What I love most about the birds is that I can hear them before I see anything. Then after a sharp curve in the path blocked mostly by the roots of a leaning cottonwood it appears: A canopy of sound and bright feathers as if someone is having a pillow fight with the rainbow. Peacocks. Doves. Parrots. Yellow canaries. Even a sad-looking ostrich. Eve and I never fail to lose our breath at the sight of it. A stain of some other world flung against the flat simmering houses of tan orange and burnt rose. Birds singing in the light.

"Let's try to get a peacock feather!" I say as we begin searching for a stick thin and long enough to fit through the wire fence keeping the birds in. The feathers collect like leaves against the edges of the cages and sometimes if we are lucky we can fish a perfect one out.

"This time try not to get one with crap on it!" Eve teases.

I crouch down low and roll up my sleeves. The ostrich turns its bulging eyes at me as if to say: *Who are you?* Batting away the crusty and feces-stained feathers I dig with the end of the stick until I find a perfect one and nudge it toward the holes in the wire.

"Careful! Don't mess it up. Slowly." Eve is peering over my shoulder.

I hold my breath and focus. I inch the feather out and grab the tip of it with my fingers.

"Wow." Eve says. "That's a good one."

I grin wide. And for a moment I forget all about Mama and the shredder and this sucky day.

"Let's keep going." Eve says.

So we walk along the ditch for the rest of the afternoon. Sometimes we talk and sometimes we stare up at the blinding blue sky lost in our own daydreams. We smile at neighbors outside with their bar-b-ques fired up. We inhale the smell of smoke and meat and celebration. And we ignore our own growling stomachs. We poke sticks into the muddy ditch water and watch crayfish scurry out. We visit a couple horses that have sauntered over to a fence. We pet their wide noses and let their gummy mouths explore our palms. Around sunset we make it back home. Mama is in her room with the TV on but the living room floor is still littered with papers.

Eve and I clean up and then make ourselves fish sticks for dinner. Around 9pm the fireworks start to go off downtown. So Eve and I climb up into the cottonwood and watch the sky. Hoping for a glimpse. But we're in the valley. We are too far away to see much.

"Well happy fricken birthday America." Eve says with a sigh. Then she grabs my hand and squeezes. And we wait. Eventually a few big ones make it to us. They light the whole sky and then fizzle out. Then we are in the dark again.

Girl Scouts

The day after the paper shredder incident is Tuesday and we are back to our summer routine. Eve leaves for work at 10am and we are both up before Mama.

"Make sure she eats. I made extra eggs." Eve whispers to me on her way out. "Oh. And let's not tell anyone about all the shredding business ok?"

"Not even Papa?" I ask.

"Especially not Papa. She seems fine now. Let's not worry him."

And even though I notice that Eve's voice catches when she says "fine" I am relieved. I promised Papa that I would look out for Mama. I'd just have to do better. Watch her even closer. Keep her safe. We'd all be fine.

After Eve leaves I heat up the eggs and make toast. I leave a covered plate for Mama on the counter and then head outside to read in the sun. Around noon I see Mama in the kitchen. I watch her make coffee and eat a dry piece of toast. Then she heads back to her room. The plate of eggs is still on the counter. At 3pm I leave for Girl Scouts. On my way out I press my ear to Mama's door until I hear her faint snores.

For three weeks I've been attending meetings just to make her happy. Wearing my stupid kelly-green vest and keeping my head down. But today when I pull up and lock my bike I feel uneasy. Like people are watching me. Like maybe they know Mama is not herself. When I enter the rec room I beeline to the craft table and pull out my songbook to work on some lyrics that have been bouncing around in my head:

I am a girl
I am a seed
I am a song
I am a weed
I am my own
I am alone
Growing growing
In this dry dry heat

I hear Mrs. Karen our troop leader yell: "Ten minutes of free time girls! And then we'll circle up." But I keep my eyes focused on the page as the room chatters with activity. The rest of the girls' voices buzz in my ears. And so focused am I on the uniform hum of their voices. So focused am I on trying to find the perfect lyrics to accompany the music of the room. That when I hear Alma call me a "dirty black orphan" I do not cry. I just look up at her standing over me with a mean smirk on her face and I open and close my mouth like a fish. I look around for help but Mrs. Karen has stepped out and the rest of the girls are gathering around to watch. Even Lydia hovers outside of the circle. Waiting to see what happens. Alma's face is twisted into a sneer. I can tell she's been waiting for this moment since I joined. Since she teased me about my "hipster-ass bike" on the first day.

"You think you're better than us?" Alma starts now. "Talking all proper like a white girl. You know you're not white right? You know you're just like the rest of us."

I look around at the rest of the troop. Twelve Latina girls. A couple of white girls including Lydia shuffling their feet in the corner. And me. A mismatched girl. *No. I do not think I am better than you.* I say in my head. *I am just me. I am a seed.* But my tongue swells in my mouth as if stung by a bee. And no words come out. I've barely spoken ten sentences to anyone the whole time I've been in the troop. Keeping to myself. *What gave me away?* I hadn't let Mama drop me off once since I started.

"Oh now you can't speak?" Alma continues. "I know all about your family. Mrs. Karen said your parents don't even look like you."

"I know who I am!" I yell back finding my voice. And then.

As if someone has forced a finger down my throat I hear myself say: "At least I know HOW to speak English you stupid Mexican."

And I feel so heavy then. *Why did I say that?!* As if someone has filled my ugly green vest with sandbags. I can barely move my arms my legs. And so when Alma calls me a dirty black orphan along with some other horrible names I do not cry. I cannot cry because even my eyes feel weighted. I grab my things and walk out slowly trying to hold my head high. And Alma yells and yells and yells in my ear and some of the other girls cheer and cheer and cheer Alma on.

QUESTIONS I HAVE FOR BLACK GIRLS LIKE ME

posted July 5th

Dear L

I got the blues

I got the blues

Like Billie and Ella

I'm so sad

They sing the news

They sing the blues

I can't sleep

I can't sleep

So I listen

I listen instead

And how many ways

Can I hear a song

Can I lose myself

In a song

Can a song find me

A lost girl

Remind me of

A singing kind of home

I got the blues

I got the blues

And how many times

Can I surrender

To the jazz

Of these women

How many times

Do I find myself

Awake at night

Hanging on

To every sad note

I am alive

I am alive

I am a searching girl

I hurt

I grow

My heart is full

Of singing ghosts

XOXO

K

In This House We Believe

On Wednesday Mama gets a call from Mrs. Karen. "Makeda!" She yells. "Get in here right now."

I slide into her bedroom. She has the TV on some loud talk show where people are booing and yelling at one another.

"Have a seat." She motions to a spot at her feet and then mutes the TV. "Do you know who that was?"

"Mrs. Karen?"

"Do you want to tell me what's going on? I never thought you'd say something so insensitive. You know that New Mexico used to be Mexico right? We don't tease people because they speak another language. This is a country of immigrants. We are not bigots. Plus. Spanish is the second most commonly spoken language in the United States so you'd be smart to learn it and respect it. Of all people Makeda. I'm really disappointed in you. I expect you to write Alma an apology."

"Me! What about her? Did Mrs. Karen tell you what Alma said to me?!"

"Yes. And Mrs. Karen assured me that Alma's parents would be getting a call too. But Makeda. You're better than your response.

I know what she said must have hurt. But you know you're not an orphan. You have us."

"She called me dirty." I say quietly.

"Well that's just mean. But honestly. You've got to be the bigger person. Mrs. Karen said that you keep to yourself and that some of the girls think you're shy. But I'm sure if you just give the troop more of a chance and maybe come out of your shell you'd make friends easier."

"Well do you have any friends?" My voice is shaking. Even my ribs seem to tremble. "You just sit in the house all day doing nothing. Why do I have to go out and make friends when you don't even have to leave your bed?!"

"Makeda that is not the same. I am the adult here. You are the child. Don't be rude. I'm sorry about what Alma said to you. But what you said is also wrong and it's offensive and we don't say those kinds of things in this family."

Mama is rubbing her temples and has her eyes squeezed shut. I can tell she's tired. "Do you remember what the sign says on our lawn?" Mama continues. "The one we brought with us from Baltimore. To let all our neighbors know what we stand for?"

I nod my head. It's hard to miss the sign. The first week we arrived Mama stomped down our long driveway to the end and then hammered the sign into the grass at the edge of our yard. The sign is white with rainbow lettering and it reads:

IN THIS HOUSE WE BELIEVE:
BLACK LIVES MATTER
WOMEN'S RIGHTS ARE HUMAN RIGHTS
NO HUMAN IS ILLEGAL
LOVE IS LOVE
KINDNESS IS EVERYTHING

"Well? Do you?" Mama is still waiting for my answer.

"Yes. I remember."

"Good. Now please go write an apology and bring it to me when you're done. We'll drop it off at the community center later this afternoon."

"I'm not going back." I manage to say. "I'll write the apology. But I'm not going to be in the troop anymore. I just won't."

"We'll talk about it later Makeda. Right now it's time to be the bigger person."

Mama unmutes the TV and I know she is done talking. I walk back to my room and slam the door but the sound is no competition for the TV. I grab a piece of white paper from my desk and a pen. I sit on my bed and stare at the blank page. Before I know it tears are falling onto the paper. I know what I said was wrong. It made my entire body heavy. But if we believe "kindness is everything" why doesn't it also matter what Alma said to me?

Dear Alma

I feel really bad for calling you stupid. I know you are very smart and I know you belong in this country. I am very sorry. I wish I could speak two languages. But you should know I didn't appreciate the names you called me. They were hurtful and I was just trying to stick up for myself.

Have a great rest of your summer.

Keda

Melody Icey

Mama skims my apology. "Good." She says.

"Did you read the whole thing?"

"Yes."

I stand by her bed and wait for her to say more but she sinks back down into the sheets. No more lectures about being the better person or knowing how to stand up for yourself in ways that don't hurt others. Instead of being annoyed with me she acts like I don't exist. I wait a few more seconds and watch Mama try to get comfortable. Her face is full of pain as if she's trying to nap on a bed of sharp things. "Makeda. Please stop hovering." She finally barks and then turns her back to me and goes to sleep. I tiptoe out and leave her door cracked.

At 4 o'clock Mama emerges from her room and drives me by the rec center. She hasn't bothered to get dressed so I leave the note in Mrs. Karen's mailbox by the front desk.

"We won't tell your father about this." Mama says on our way back. "But don't let it happen again."

"Ok." I say knowing we probably won't speak to Papa until the middle of next week anyway since he's traveling in some remote town in South Korea now. And that Mama will probably forget all about this by that time. She's been forgetting a lot these days.

I glance up front. Mama's freckles seem to jump off her face in the rearview mirror. Her cheeks are almost raw red. As if she is sunburnt and blushing all at the same time. She's wearing a floppy straw hat and has pulled her hair back into a greasy ponytail that hangs down her back like a sad ribbon. I have the urge to cut it off. *What's the point of having hair like that if you're not going to enjoy or take care of it?* I pat my own hair. It's grown out a few inches and even though Stormy told me to come back two weeks after "the chop" Mama hasn't made another appointment in weeks. So I try as much as I can to take care of it myself. To pick it out with the Afro pick Mama had in her tub full of my old hair stuff. So that it's even. But the back has grown out too much and in the mirror I can see I need Stormy's help. If my hair could be long and smooth like Mama's maybe girls wouldn't tease me. Maybe I wouldn't feel like such a twisted ball of yarn all the time. Maybe I'd still be in Girl Scouts. Or in 6th grade at El Rio. Maybe nobody would call me names.

"Should we stop by the Melody Icey and surprise your sister?" Mama's voice breaks into my thoughts.

"Right now?" I look down at my stained shorts and faded

pink tank top. And then I glance at Mama's holey sweatpants. "Maybe we should go tomorrow?"

"Nonsense. We're already out. I want to see where Eve's been disappearing to all these weeks."

When we pull up to the parking lot it's packed. Mama circles the lot until we find a spot and then we walk up to the entrance. I take a place at the end of the line but Mama pushes her way through the crowd. "Excuse me. My daughter works here. Excuse me. We'll only be a moment." She keeps repeating as if she has VIP access. "Come on Makeda. What are you doing back there?" She yells from up ahead and the whole line turns to look at me.

"What are you doing here?" I hear Eve's voice as Mama reaches the front.

"There she is. Look at you! Hard at work. And in uniform too!" Mama squeals. "How cute is that little hat."

Eve is wearing all red with a white apron and a little cap on her head that looks like an upside-down cone.

"You look like a sad unicorn." I can't help but giggle. In fact all the other employees do too. The upside-down ice cream cone hats slipping down over their eyes as they bend over to scoop ice cream from the enormous freezers.

"Haha. Very funny." Eve says. "Keda don't even get me started on your outfit today."

"Well I think it's cute." Mama says again. Eyeing the tubs full of ice cream. "I'm very proud of you Eve. At least one of my daughters is making the best out of her summer."

There go my ribs again. Trembling. *Did Mama drive here just to make me feel worse?*

"Mama. You're holding up the line. What do you want?" Eve has no time for praise. She's very busy. The line behind us is growing impatient.

Mama orders a waffle cone with a triple scoop of cookies and cream. "I only had toast for breakfast." She says. "So make the scoops extra large."

"Maybe you want to eat something else when you get home?" Eve throws me a nervous look. "Like with protein or something?"

"Mmmmh this is soo delicious!" Mama ignores Eve and is already devouring her cone.

I get a double scoop of mint chocolate chip on a sugar cone. We sit at a table by the counter so we can watch Eve in action. Mama doesn't look at me once. Every now and then she sighs with admiration at Eve. "She gets her social charm and stage presence from me." Mama says to no one in particular. Watching as Eve jokes with a customer and his daughter. Halfway through eating my ice cream I get a stomachache.

"Better eat the rest before it melts." Mama pushes.

"I'm full." I say. "I kinda feel like I'll throw up if I take another bite."

"Well next time get a smaller scoop. There are kids all over the world who don't have the luxury of wasting food. You're lucky you know."

"I know." I manage to eat a few more bites. Then I just let the ice cream cone melt in the sun. My hands sticky with guilt.

Never Forget

That night the Georgia Belles show up but they sound different. Their voices somewhere in between shouting and singing. I toss and turn in my bed and fall in and out of darkness. Around 2am sticky hands pull me from my sleep.

Did you forget about us? The Georgia Belles fill the whole room with their new noise. At first they are sweet sisters. They tell me all about Atlanta. How the light leans crooked off of rooftops at sunset how peach cobbler is supposed to taste.

We know your real mama. The one that gave you away. They sing.

What does she look like? Is she pretty? I sing back.

You know she looks regular. Like a regular black woman.

But I do not know anymore. I know the pink color of the Sandia Mountains at sunset.

I know the roundness of my own dark cheeks. But I don't really know any regular black women. *What do they sound like what do they feel like what do they wear to church on Sundays?* The questions spill out of my mouth like silk.

The questions make an intricate web on the walls. But the Georgia Belles whisk them away with their hands. *Too many questions*. They scold. *You're not listening*. I am listening. I want them to leave. I want everyone to leave me alone.

I close my eyes and count to one hundred. I open my eyes to find the Georgia Belles even closer now. Sitting on the edge of my bed. The Georgia Belles getting their sticky hands all over my yellow sheets. The Georgia Belles throwing tall tales around the room.

The Georgia Belles laughing when I yell: *Go away!* The Georgia Belles harmonizing and sing-yelling back: *Don't be mad just 'cause you talk like a white girl. A spoiled little white girl who never gets slapped.*

It is raining. It is the first time in weeks. The Georgia Belles sway to the window and block the breeze. I am so thirsty. I'm all mixed up in my bedsheets. My cheeks are chewed bloody. *Your mama didn't want you 'cause you're ugly*. They roar.

I want to kill them. *Your mama told me you looked like a prune when you were born. A shriveled black prune and that's why she gave you away*. I do not know. I'm all mixed up in my sheets.

I don't care about HER. I don't need her. Go away! I yell.

The Georgia Belles move from the window and stand silent over me. They smell of hospital sheets and wet bark. *We told you not to forget*. They belt.

I cannot look away. The Georgia Belles lean in looking like all the pretty but messy parts of a storm. *Never forget*. They hiss. Then the Georgia Belles slap me into morning with their sticky sticky hands.

The Boy Book

Mama and I are so tired the next day that we forget we are hosting the end-of-year homeschool party on Saturday. It's Eve who reminds us and somehow we get the house in order just in time. The day of the party Mama orders six pizzas from Sweet Tomato and Eve brings home two tubs of ice cream for the party. Everyone else brings a dish or a dessert to share. Mama sets up a big table on the back porch. She and the other parents hang out while we run around the yard and play games. I wait for Huck to arrive but Mr. John pulls up alone. "Huck's away at Model United Nations camp." He tells us. And my heart sinks. So much for Huck ever remembering me now. I probably won't see him again until the fall.

By 8pm the party ends and everyone heads home. Mr. John stays to help clean up the back porch. As he is leaving he turns to me and says: "Huck wanted me to tell you 'Bye. And have a great summer.' He was sorry to miss this."

"Oh. Thanks. I hope he has fun at Model UN camp."

I want to ask Mr. John what Huck's email address is. *Maybe we can write each other messages?* But Mr. John is out the door before I get a chance. *So Huck was thinking about me after all?* I feel heat rise in my cheeks. *What could this mean?* I look at the clock. It's already 10pm in Baltimore. Too late to call Lena. I really could use our boy book right now.

The boy book is a black journal that Lena and I used to share. It has the name of every boy we've had a crush on including celebrities like Prince Harry and Jaden Smith. When I was still living in Baltimore Lena and I passed it back and forth on the weekends like a piece of top secret evidence. When we found out I was moving we buried it in a Ziploc bag in her backyard for safe keeping. Under the name of each boy crush is his identifying information and a neatly printed T-chart listing his pros and cons. After listing the pros and cons of each boy we go through them together and rate each pro or con on a scale of 1 to 10 of how important it is to us: 10 = very important and 1 = not important. Then we add the numbers up. If the pros outnumber the cons we know it is true love. If the cons outweigh the pros then we know that the boy is trash and not worth our time.

I head to the computer and start a new post. I know Lena will check it in the morning.

posted Saturday July 9th

L

I'm so mad we buried the boy book because I could really use it. We'll have to dig it up next time I see you. I hope I can visit soon. These homeschool kids are ok but no one compares to you. Or the adventures we used to have together.

Well there's really only one person who has my eye. Maybe you can help me figure out if it's worth it?

Huck Andrew Peterson

Age: 12

Hair: Black

Skin: Tan

Eyes: Light brown with flecks of gold

Muscles: Kinda

PROS	CONS
Can recite every country and capital in North and South America by memory	Obsessed with geography
Is taller than me and in 7th grade	Needs to shave his upper lip
Has a cool room with maps and stuff and has lived here his whole life	Awkward and shy
Likes to read like me	Is a spoiled only child and can be a big baby when he gets mad
Has a birthmark shaped like a pear on his left arm	Has annoying parents
Is homeschooled like me and can be really sweet if you get to know him	Might not like black girls

Fireball

Is no longer an angel. The rest of the baby chicks have turned into sweet midsized hens. But Fireball is a rooster and he is the worst of them all. He is a miniature terror with mean eyes and feathers the color of burning embers and I secretly hope the wild dogs will eat him alive. On Sunday morning Mama wakes us up yelling from the kitchen: "Fireball got out of the pen again!" She's been grumpy at me since I told her I wasn't going back to Girl Scouts. After grumbling and washing the sleep out of our eyes Eve and I dress ourselves for battle. We know better than to ignore her when she gets this way. We put on thick jeans and big rubber galoshes and puffy winter coats for protection (even though it is July) and then for extra dramatics I strap on Papa's racquetball goggles.

"You girls look ridiculous!" Mama says over her coffee mug. "He's just a rooster. You can't even see properly in those goggles."

"Why don't you try catching him then!" Eve yells back. "Come on let's get this over with." She says to me.

I love to run. Especially next to Eve. The two of us scramble around the yard arms outstretched trying to herd Fireball back into the pen or into a corner so that we can grab him by the plume as he squawks and bites. I roar and charge at him as if I am a gladiator or a bull or Joan of Arc. I know I am the bravest. That I am the one. Who cares if those girls didn't like me. Who cares if Mama is mad. The whole world will see. One day I'll move to a big city with diners and park benches and tall buildings. I'll rush through the streets with my songbook and binoculars and see it all with my own eyes.

"Grab him!" Eve yells as she falls behind. And I find myself alone in a corner staring Fireball down. Alone in a corner with the morning sky cracking yolk-light all over my head.

"You stupid rooster!" I yell adjusting my goggles ready to pounce. "I would eat you myself if I could."

Upside Down

After we argue about Fireball and get him back in the pen. Mama does not get out of bed for three days. Not to make herself coffee or toast. Not to drive us to the library or grocery store. Not even to get the mail or scoop packages off the front porch. I'm pretty sure it's my fault she's so sad this time. I just can't seem to do anything right these days.

When Papa FaceTimes on Wednesday morning Eve and I prop Mama's laptop up in her bed so Papa can see her. She sits up and we crowd in around her so we all fit on the screen. He's calling from Hakone which is a city to the southwest of Tokyo in Japan. He shows us a view of Mount Fuji from his hotel window.

"Yes. I've been there before Daniel. Remember. When I was eleven. I think I played the Mendelssohn."

"I know love. But the girls have never seen it."

Mama seems to lose interest in the conversation then as we give Papa quick updates on our life. Mama keeps her eyes open but I can tell she is somewhere else. She doesn't say one word about me quitting Girl Scouts or about Alma. She doesn't even brag about Eve's job. I can feel that Papa is worried too because he's talking to us in an exaggerated happy tone. Almost as if we are babies.

"And is everyone taking care of themselves? Why don't you go out today? Treat yourself to a movie? Maybe go to the park. Have an adventure!"

"Daniel. I have a splitting headache." Mama says finally. "Can we talk later?"

"Sure love. Just five more weeks and then I'll be home. Hang in there."

"Uh-huh." Mama says already handing the laptop back to Eve.

We exit the room and stand in the hallway. Eve holds the computer up to our faces.

"Girls." Papa says in a voice that sounds much more like his own. "If she's not out of bed by tomorrow evening you need to let me know. And if it's an emergency you are to call 911 and then your aunt Sarah in Colorado. She can get to you quicker than I can."

"It's ok Papa." Eve says. "We've got this under control." But she bites her lip and furrows her brow when she says this. I feel my throat get dry. Part of me feels guilty for adding to Mama's stress lately but another part of me wants to run into her room throw the covers off of her and yell: GET UP. YOU ARE THE MOTHER HERE. GET UP.

When we hang up with Papa Eve motions for me to come to her room. "Shut the door." She says.

"What is it?" I say. "You're scaring me." Eve hasn't invited me into her room in forever. I look around now trying to memorize the mess: heaps of clothes and magazines. Piles of makeup and lip gloss on her dresser. A wall of pictures behind her bed with her friends from Baltimore and some from here. Her Melody Icey uniform hanging off her bedpost.

"Listen. You probably don't remember the last time Mama was like this. You were too little. But now you're older. And we both need to look out for her ok?"

"Ok." I say. "But you said we should leave her alone last time. Stay out of her way?"

"I mean. She's going to be fine. She's so dramatic sometimes. It's annoying when she gets like this." Eve is talking too fast. "But we just need to keep an eye on her and keep her happy. Like Papa said. She'll snap out of it. But we need to be in this together ok? It sucks that Papa's not here but he's never here you know?"

"Ok." I start again. "But should we call Aunt Sarah? I mean maybe we need help—"

"No. No way. We can handle this."

I gulp. "Ok." I say. "I'll try."

"Ok good." Eve jumps onto her bed and starts texting. "I'm

going to tell work I'm sick and can't come in today. I'm already late." She mumbles.

I stand in the middle of her room like a statue. *It's my fault. My fault. My fault.* I wait for Eve to offer me a spot next to her on the bed. For her to suggest we go take a walk again or play a game or sing a song but she just looks up and says: "Do you need something?"

And I know our talk is over.

I head back to my room. I look out the window. It is sunny. A beautiful day. Everything feels upside down and Eve's behavior is confusing. One minute she wants us to "be in this together" and the next she acts like I'm the one annoying her. Being a needy baby. I didn't ask for any of this. I should be outside. In the sunshine.

So I load up my backpack with sheets sticks books and canned goods. I dump my bag into an old rusty red wagon. Then I drag the wagon around the yard until I find a good place to build a tent fort.

"You're a freak!" Eve yells from the house when she emerges from her room hours later and sees me sitting in my tent fort reading and eating my dinner from an open can of chili. "What do you think this is Coachella?"

And I stick out my tongue and yell back: "At least I have an imagination!"

In my tent fort I am the boss. I am in charge. I take care of myself. I am going places and nobody can stop me.

QUESTIONS I HAVE FOR BLACK GIRLS LIKE ME

posted July 12th

Dear K

Sorry I have not written you in a while! I've been traveling for gym meets and next week I'm off to gymnastics camp for a month. I hope I will be able to write you on here while I am away. But just know that if I don't I will write you as soon as I am back in August. Promise.

I really loved the song you posted about having the blues. Even if it was kinda depressing. LOL. Did something happen again? Wish I could meet you for ice cream and cheer you up. I miss you.

I hope you are making friends in that homeschool group. They all sound . . . interesting. But Huck seems cool. I mean. You know me. Go big or go home! LOL. I think you should go for it. Why not?

I've been super busy. I'm competing more than ever. Coach Asia says if I really want to make it as a gymnast I can. But I have to be even more committed. So I'm at the gym every day. I miss having you at my meets. Cheering me on.

Here's a question I have: Why do black girls have to work ten times harder at anything we do?

Coach Asia told me I can be great. Like she was. But that people will always have eyes on me. Expect me to be perfect. Because there are still people in the world who really believe that black people are lazy. That as a black gymnast I am going to be "under a microscope." Sometimes before a meet I feel like throwing up when I see all the people in the stands. Staring down at me.

Ok. Well. I have to go. I'll try to write you one more time before camp. Oh man. Camp is gonna kick my butt.

Your BFF

L

Fire

My songs are not enough. The nighttime pulses and a heat I cannot control spreads over my body like brushfire. Later that night I throw my blankets into a pile on the floor. I lie on my stomach and press my chest into the coolness of my bottom sheet. I try with all my strength to ignore the growing pains in my legs. To not be ashamed of the ways I am changing. Nobody told me that growing up hurts. I smash my face into the pillow so that I can barely breathe. Not even Lena's posts or thoughts of Huck or the feeling of the wind trailing its fingers on my back will make me feel better. So I thrash and thrash and thrash. And ache and ache and ache. And I curse my body for being so difficult. For being a piece of crumbling char that does not know how to light itself.

"DO YOU LOVE IT? I LOVE IT! I GOT IT AT ROSS!"

The next morning Mama jumps out of bed with a smile on her face and yells down the hall: "Let's get the hell out of here girls! Your father was right. We do need to treat ourselves and have some fun."

"See?" Eve yells across the hall as we get dressed. "Told you she'd snap out of it."

We grab our purses and sunglasses and march out the door in a parade of excitement and I sit in the back seat of the minivan feeling just like Eliza Doolittle from *My Fair Lady.* Ready to make my public debut. We arrive at Ross and rush through the sliding doors into the air-conditioned building. Eve beelines for the juniors racks while Mama runs her fingers over shiny pots and colored glass jars in the housewares aisle.

I like to try on formal dresses. Ones I can wear during piano recitals or on the rare occasion I go to the symphony to see Papa play cello. I fill my arms with puffed sleeves and velvet bodices and skirts dotted with sequins and head to the dressing room. And then I twirl and twirl and twirl in the mirror until Mama comes in with another dress to try on and the attendant says:

"Oh no ma'am there's just some black girl in there." And then the fun is over.

"That's my daughter!" Mama storms past the attendant into my dressing room. And I understand why it makes her so mad. It makes me mad too. But in the car on the way home Mama stares ahead with tears in the corners of her eyes and mutters to herself: "People just can't see past color can they?"

And I feel like punching her. I am the one with the color after all. I am the one.

"Mama. Calm down. That lady is ignorant. Don't get upset ok? We're fine. Keda's fine. Right?" Eve turns to look at me from the passenger seat. Her eyes plead to not make Mama any more upset. "We were having such a nice day." Eve continues. "Don't let some random ruin it."

"Are you really ok Makeda?" Mama says then looking at me in the mirror. "You know I'm just so on edge these days. I can't believe things like this still happen."

I want to tell Mama I am not fine. And how does "not seeing color" even make sense? I see my color every day. In the mirror. At the store when eyes follow me around wondering if I'm stealing or who I belong to. I see my color in the eyes of my peers. When they spit names at me or compliments they think are nice. I see my color in my dreams. In the songs that the Georgia Belles sing to me. In my nightmares. I can't be without color. It is me. For better or for worse. This is me.

"I'm fine." I say through gritted teeth. And then it's as if we can all breathe again. Some of us easier than others.

QUESTIONS I HAVE FOR BLACK GIRLS LIKE ME

posted July 17th

Dear L

Have fun at camp! But PLEASE write me as soon as you can. LOL. I mean. I know you'll be working hard but I am your BFF. And yeah. I know what you mean about having "all eyes on you." Sometimes I feel like I am under a microscope. And then other times like I am completely invisible. But just remember: You are strong. You can do anything. I know you can.

I wish I was going somewhere fun this summer. Instead I am here. In this stupid desert. Hanging out with my mom. Who apparently doesn't "see color." ***EYE ROLL*** Anyway. Long story. Just be happy that you get some time away from your parents. Sigh. I miss talking to you. Don't forget about me ok?

xoxo
K

Flying

Two days later at 4am Mama wakes us up. "Little birds." She chirps. "It's time for an adventure. Time to fly."

Her face leaning over me in bed looks like a glowing planet. She smiles with all her strong teeth and I can tell she's washed her hair because her braids are tight and neat and smell of lavender.

"What time is it? I have to work early." Eve grumbles from the darkness of her room.

"Just after 4am. And don't worry about work. We'll call them from the road."

"Where are we going?" I finally find my words as I sit up and stretch.

"It's a surprise. Your dad's not the only one who gets to go on a trip this summer. Now hurry! I want to beat traffic. This is going to be the perfect getaway for all of us. Everything is going to be better."

Maybe it's the joyful tone in Mama's voice that makes us not ask questions. Maybe it's because this is the first time she's said "it's going to be better" since we moved or the fact that she's already packed the car and made us each a snack bag. Or maybe we are just too tired to register what is happening. But faster than we can say "Mama no" we're on the highway driving away. The city wrapped in slumber. Mama's hands steady on the wheel. Her flip-flops tossed on the passenger seat as her bare foot presses on the gas pedal. All the windows open. A gritty wind ripping at her pale always sunburnt skin. And it feels good. To be on the road again. Mama driving so fast and straight and free. Driving until edges of the landscape begin to bleed sunrise. Until a sky so clear and sharp greets us with a new day.

Boulder

Seven hours later (with one quick bathroom stop and a drive through lunch) we arrive in Boulder Colorado. Just outside of the city Mama turns down a dirt path and winds the van up a steep road. We are at the foot of the Rocky Mountains. The aspen trees stand tall at the edges of the road and the circles of black on their white trunks blink at us like eyes. Mama is glowing. She hasn't slept all night but she is full of chatter as we wind up and up and up. Higher and higher into the mountains.

"We're almost there. Do you girls recognize it here?" Mama asks.

"I do." says Eve. "We came here when I was little right?"

"Kinda." I say. Sticking my hand out the window to feel the strength of the mountain air against my palm.

"Yes. Eve I think you were five and Makeda was still a toddler. And I used to come here too. As a little girl. With Aunt Sarah and your grandma Esther. We've been renting this cabin for years. We're lucky I got a reservation so last minute. Thankfully someone just canceled."

"Are there bunk beds?" I ask. "I remember bunk beds."

Mama laughs. "Yes! There's a loft above the main room with bunks. That's where you'll be sleeping. Last time you were too young to climb the ladder to the loft. You slept in the bedroom with me and Papa."

Mama pulls off the main road onto an even narrower dirt road until we arrive at the cabin. It is made of golden logs and sits on the edge of a slope so that the back of the cabin looks down and out over a sea of trees and rocks.

"How long are we staying?" Eve says checking the service bars on her phone. "I was supposed to work all week. And who's taking care of the chickens?"

"Oh come on. You're no fun Eve." Mama says stopping the car and jumping out. "Work will still be there when we get back. I asked Mr. John to take care of the chickens while we're away. Let's just live in the moment and soak up this scenery ok?" And with that Mama skips into the cabin.

"How would you know? You've never even been able to keep a real job." Eve mutters after Mama.

I turn in my seat and look back at Eve. The expression on her face is somewhere between amused and annoyed. "Are you ok?" I ask.

"Yeah. I just don't get it. She seems so happy. But I didn't realize we were driving all the way to another state. It's a little weird right?"

"A little."

"Well. At least my phone seems to still be working even though we're in the middle of nowhere."

"WHAT ARE YOU STILL DOING IN THE VAN?!" Mama is waving from the front door. "GET IN HERE. LET'S GO FOR A HIKE. THE VIEWS ARE GLORIOUS."

"Come on." Eve says then climbing out. "Maybe this is what we all need."

"Yeah." I say. "It could be fun." And we grab our bags and meet Mama inside.

After

We take a mini hike. After that we drive down the mountain for groceries and ice cream. After that we eat loaded baked potatoes and watch the sun set on the back deck. Mama jumps up and says: "I think it's time for a show. Let's put some music on."

Eve and I grab our dinner plates and head inside where we drop them into the sink and then run up to the loft to change into our sweatpants. Below us. In the main room. Mama moves aside a leather armchair and then pushes a small love seat into a corner. Then she rolls up the rug to make a dance space. She lights a few candles and then plugs her phone into the speakers.

"Ladies and gentlemen!" She announces. "I present to you 'The Dance of the Sugar Plum Fairies'!" It is one of our favorite songs from Tchaikovsky's *The Nutcracker.* Even Eve can't deny it. We look down and see Mama has already started twirling around the room. So Eve and I make our way down the stairs and Mama hands us each one of her silk scarves. The ones she uses to pad her violin in its case. Then Mama takes her place conducting us from the armchair with one hand as she pours herself a big glass of wine. Eve and I curtsy in the center of the room. Then. As the celesta begins its bell-like tune we spring into an intricate dance of tiptoeing and spinning and leaping around the room.

"Yes girls! That's it! Toes pointed. Tummies in. Legs graceful and sharp. Bravo. Bellissima. Wonderful!" Mama cheers. "And now twirl! Twirl! Don't stop." And Eve and I spin and slide around the floor in our socks as fast and as gracefully as we can. Bumping into one another. Our tongues sticking out of the corners of our mouths in concentration. Until we are so dizzy and out of breath we fall to the ground giggling and panting as Mama gives us a standing ovation.

"Girls." She gasps. Downing the rest of her glass. "What fun we're going to have here. Who needs your father?"

And I almost believe her.

When she tucks us into bed hours later (even though we are both too old for this). Her two long braids fall onto my face and I inhale the tingly smell of her lavender shampoo now mixed with the scent of spruce tree sap. I want to wrap her braids around my neck like a scarf. I want to climb up them like she is Rapunzel until I am in her arms. *Don't leave me.* But I don't say this. I let her kiss my forehead and then I burrow under the covers.

"Good night my little birds." She turns off the light and heads down the steep ladder. Eve is already snoring on the top bunk. I pull out my flashlight and a flat speckled rock I found on our hike from under my pillow. I rub it in my palms and then drag it lightly across my arms. My stomach. My neck. I put it in my mouth and hold it like an egg on my tongue. I suck on the silk of it and then take it out. Only to watch it shine and then turn to chalk again. Downstairs Mama's phone is ringing and then it stops. Mama must have silenced it. I hear her uncorking more wine. I fall asleep to the thought of her taking out her braids. Her hair so long and thick it joins the moonlight outside and floats on the top of the darkness like a path of glittering lily pads.

The River

I dream a new dream at the cabin that night. I am in a house and it is hot. Sticky hot. I am slicing peaches on a countertop and in another room a woman is singing along with the radio. There are no words to her song. Or if there are words they are words that I can't understand. As I finish the last peach the house begins to shake. The house breaks in half and a deep river gushes through the middle. I grab the knife and run out into an orchard. I see the shadow of a woman waving her arms from the river. She waves and waves and waves and then she smiles. Sinks. And is gone.

When I wake up I am drenched in sweat. The cabin is dark and seems to quiver with the noise of Mama's and Eve's snoring. I sneak down the ladder and get myself a glass of water. I tiptoe past Mama who has fallen asleep on the love seat still dressed. Her legs flung over the sides like a rag. At the kitchen window I stare hard into the dark and watch the moon dressing herself against the curtain of trees. What I can't seem to shake about the dream is the back of her hand. Waving calmly. As if she knew all along the river was coming. I lick my own hand and taste dirt. I gulp down the water and then sneak back upstairs. And after I'm back in bed. The water settling in my stomach. All I can think of is peaches. How if only I could fill my mouth with their flesh I might not be hungry anymore. How the disappearing woman looked both like Mama and someone I've never met.

Needles & Yarn

Even though we are exhausted from our first day at the cabin we set out early again the next morning.

"We need to busy our hands!" Mama tells us as she winds down the mountain into the city at 8am.

"I thought this was supposed to be relaxing?" Eve says.

"It is! What's more relaxing than knitting?"

"Um I dunno. Reading a book in the sun. Swimming in the river. Watching movies and napping. Literally anything else."

"Makeda." Mama continues. Ignoring Eve. "I'll teach you how to knit. It's really easy when you get the hang of it. And it feels so satisfying to make something from scratch."

I don't remind Mama that she's already taught me how to knit. I'm not very good but two years ago I made a lumpy scarf the color of sea glass. I just nod my head. She's been so happy. Why spoil it? I could use a refresher anyway.

The store we pull up to is called Needles & Yarn. Mama bounds inside and instantly starts pulling hand-dyed yarns and wooden needles off the shelves.

"Oooh. What's this?" She asks the clerk. Rubbing her cheeks against a fluffy ball of cotton candy pink yarn.

"Well that's one of our luxury yarns. It's made of one hundred percent super merino wool. It's spun chunky and light to resemble clouds."

"My word it's divine!" Mama's eyes light up. "Girls. Come feel this."

We hustle over and take turns rubbing the ball of yarn on our cheeks.

"It really is like a cloud." Eve says. "Cool."

"It's so soft. I just want to eat it." I giggle.

"We'll take it." Mama almost yells with excitement.

"Just the one?" The clerk confirms.

"Oh no. We'll take all of it. How many balls do you have?"

"Mama! All of them?" I look at the price tag. One ball costs $30. "What are we going to do with all of it?"

"Makeda. Please don't bring that anxious energy in here. We're treating ourselves. Just like your father said. Money is not an issue."

I look at Eve. But she's texting her friends. Her face is buried in her screen.

"I'll just hold all these up at the register for you." The clerk says gathering up the thirty balls of cotton candy cloud yarn. "So you can keep shopping."

And Mama keeps going. She tornadoes around the store yelling to no one in particular and laughing at odd times and when I try to ask her a question she only half answers.

"Mama! You're making us dizzy." Eve hisses. "Slow down."

"Eve! Just relax. We're paying customers. We can do what we want."

"Whatever. I'll be outside." Eve says to Mama. And then to me: "Make sure she doesn't buy the whole store."

I am trying to relax but Eve's warning makes my hands sweat. I try to enjoy the store with Mama but she is hard to keep up with. By the time Mama is finished she's filled two additional baskets full of yarn and supplies and has picked us all an artisan crochet pouch to keep our needles in. I stand behind Mama as the clerk rings up our items. Each time she scans something I feel a tingle in the pit of my stomach. *It's too much. We don't need all this.* Voices sing in my head.

"Your total is one thousand three hundred seventy-four dollars and fifty-seven cents. Will that be cash or card?"

"Swipe away!" Mama laughs handing over her Visa. "It's so worth it. We're going to make so many beautiful things. Aren't we peach?" She says looking down at me but not really looking at me.

"Yeah. Sure." I say. "I can't wait."

And Mama kisses me on the head. "Grab the bags!" She calls. "Next stop is the mall. You both need some new clothes."

No More Sweatpants and Frumpy Shirts

At the mall Mama insists that we get all new outfits for the fall. We run around J. C. Penney and Mama throws item after item into our cart. By the time we get to the dressing room the cart is overflowing with dresses and jeans and tops and more. I am so excited about my new outfits that I twirl and twirl in the dressing room. I'm finally getting a couple formal dresses to wear to concerts. Since we left our last shopping trip at Ross without getting anything.

But just as I am practicing a curtsy in a red dress Eve sticks her head into my stall and frowns at me. "Keda!" She hisses. "This is not a game. We need to tell Mama we don't need all of this. I mean. You know I love shopping. But this. This is cray cray."

"Mama says we're treating ourselves." I try. But I know something is not right.

"Makeda don't be a baby. You know that's not what's happening here. Take off that dress and put it back. I'll try to sneak some of the other things in the cart back onto the racks."

"I'm not a baby!" I hiss at Eve. But she's already left my stall.

I tear off the dress I am wearing and shove it under the bench in the dressing room. *It's not fair! It's not fair!* My head screams. *Why can't we just have a fun shopping day!* But then I help Eve put some of the things in our cart back while Mama is trying on dresses of her own.

Mama still spends $500 on clothes for us. Then she buys herself two new concert gowns that cost about $300 each.

"Do you have a concert coming up?" I ask.

"No. But I will. This trip is the recharge I need. My head is so clear. I know I can book some gigs if I just focus and practice. And also if I look good! No more sweatpants and frumpy shirts.

"Who wants a makeover?" Mama says then. Beelining for the Origins store after we leave J. C. Penney. Mama doesn't wait for an answer. She plops herself into a chair at the vanity station. "Can you do all of us?" Mama says pointing to Eve and me standing bashfully in the doorway.

"Sure can." The makeup artist coos. "We've got some great natural options for all of your complexions." But that's a lie. When she gets to me all she does is rub some dusty gold eye shadow on my lids and give me some cotton candy pink gloss that makes me look like a sad Barbie. She doesn't even try to match my skin for foundation or blush.

"You don't need that stuff anyway!" Eve whispers. When she sees the salty look on my face. "Your skin is perfect."

I roll my eyes at her. “Sure.” I say. But my makeover only takes like ten minutes. While Mama and Eve sit in the chair for at least twenty minutes each. Trying on all kinds of creams and colors and options.

In the end Mama buys herself a whole new set of moisturizer foundation concealer eye shadow mascara and lipstick. Then she buys Eve and me each a couple of lip glosses and eye shadows. I lose track of how much money we’ve spent. By 3pm we are starving. We convince Mama to let us buy pretzels and sit for a few moments as we eat them. After five minutes Mama leaps up. “Alright. Are we done? How about we get pedicures?”

“I thought you said pedicures were unhygienic? You never let us get our nails done.” Eve says still sitting. Finishing the last bite of her pretzel.

“Not your fingernails. You need to keep those short for playing piano. But getting our toes done every once in a blue moon won’t hurt.”

“What about craft day?” I ask. “When are we going back to the cabin to watch movies and knit?”

“Oh the cabin will be there! Girls come on. You can’t be pooping out on me already. This is our fun girls’ trip. We are getting pedicures and that is that. We are having fun. Fun! Fun! Fun!”

Safe

When we finally make it back from shopping it's dark. We eat peanut butter and jelly sandwiches for dinner. Mama dumps all the yarn and clothes onto the main room floor and sorts through it. Then she shows me how to cast on stitches to start a scarf. Soon she gets frustrated with the awkward way I hold the needles and gives up on me. Eve showers and then we put on some British show that Mama and Eve love but I think is kinda boring. But all that matters is that we are together and sitting still. Before I know it I fall asleep.

Eve's phone rings and rings and rings in the loft above. I open my eyes. It's still dark. Mama has left me sleeping on the love seat. Covered in a heavy blanket. I strain my ears but there is no movement from Mama's room. I get up. I climb up the loft ladder and stand on the lip of the bottom bunk until I am eye level with Eve. She snores in my face and then flips over. I reach softly under her pillow and pull out her phone. I see Papa's face lit up on the screen. I scoot down the loft ladder and into the bathroom next to Mama's room. I reach and reach and reach for the cord that hangs from the naked bulb and turns on the light but I can't find it. Papa's face flashes and flashes in the dark. I hit ANSWER and wait.

"Hello? Eve is that you? I've been calling and calling. Why can't I see your face? It's all dark. Where are you?"

"It's me!" I whisper into the phone. "I can't find the light. We were all sleeping."

"Little scoop! It's so good to hear your voice. Are you ok?"

"I'm fine. Sleepy. Why are you calling so late?"

"I've been trying to reach all of you for two days. I've been calling and calling your mother but she hasn't picked up. I even called the house line. And so now Eve. What's going on? Where are you? Is everyone safe?"

Standing in the blue-lit dark in the dead of the night. In the middle of the Rocky Mountains. Far away from any kind of home. *Am I safe?* I thought so. But then why does my jaw lock? Why does hearing Papa's worried voice make this whole girls' trip feel different? I open the bathroom door and peer out into the main room. The floor is still littered with yarn and clothes and makeup and now half-started knitting projects. There is a huge pile of unwashed dishes in the sink. And Mama has forgotten to close the cabin door. It hangs open like a crooked mouth and moonlight spills in.

"Are you still there? Makeda. Can you take me to Mama?"

"I'm here." I say. "We're fine. We just treated ourselves to a girls' trip. Like you said. Mama's idea. We're in the mountains."

"You're camping? What mountains? Your mother should have told me. I almost got on a plane when I didn't hear back."

"We're in a cabin. In Boulder. The one we used to come to I guess. We're fine. We're having fun. I think we're going home in a few days."

"She drove you all the way to Colorado! Can you wake Mama up? I want to check in. I know it's late. I'm worried. Are you sure you and your sister are ok? That Mama's ok?"

"YES! WE ARE FINE." I shout softly into the phone. The baby hairs on my arms are standing up. I start to pull and twist at the messy curls at the back of my neck. *If you're so worried about us being with Mama why did you leave in the first place?* I want to scream. But I don't. I just twist tighter at my curls.

"Ok. Will you promise to call me tomorrow? When Eve and Mama get up? No matter what time it is here. I'll be waiting."

"Where are you?" I ask. "We don't even know where you are either."

"I'm in Tokyo. And Mama knows where I am. She has all of my trip details in her email."

"Oh. Ok. Well we'll call you tomorrow. I have to go."

"Makeda. Wait. Do you think I should come home early? I think maybe this trip is too long."

“Honestly.” I hear myself saying. In what sounds like someone else’s voice. “We don’t need you. We’re having fun. Just enjoy your tour. I gotta go. Talk tomorrow.”

Before he can say anything else I hit END CALL. I shake the dark of the bathroom off of me. I shut the front door and lock it. I slip back into my bed. Then I keep my eyes open until the sun comes up.

Practice Makes Perfect

"Papa wants to hear you play something on the piano." Mama is making pancakes in the kitchen when I get up. She holds Eve's phone away from her like it's a snake and I see Papa's face again. Now it's dark where he is in the world.

"Good morning little scoop!" He winks talking in that fake cheery voice again. "Long time no see."

"But it's not even tuned!" I protest. Motioning to the upright piano in the corner of the cabin that looks like it hasn't been touched in a hundred years. "I think there are cobwebs on it."

Eve appears from the bathroom in a towel. "Don't ever take my phone like that again." She yells at me.

"Eve. Don't get mad at Makeda. I'm glad she picked up last night. It's nice to see all of my girls together having fun this morning." Papa says.

"Well you should get Makeda her own phone. That one is supposed to be mine." Eve grabs a banana and heads up to the loft to get dressed.

"Makeda. Just play something quick." Mama says again. I

shuffle over to the old Yamaha and lift the heavy cover up. Dust coats my hands. The keys feel cold and unfamiliar.

"She's getting into position with the speed of a snail." Mama yells into the phone. Placing it on top of the piano. I prop the phone up against the wall and take a deep breath. I get through a few bars and then fumble my notes. My fingers stiff and heavy with sleep.

"You're getting better." Papa lies. "But it sounds like you've skipped a few days. You don't want to get behind on your lessons."

"Well. We're on vacation." I say.

"Just keep working. Remember practice makes perfect."

"Nobody else is practicing." I mumble. *Why is this whole conversation all of a sudden about me? Why isn't he talking to Mama? She's the one he's worried about.*

Mama grabs back the phone. "Honestly Daniel" she starts "we are fine and having fun. I'll make sure we all practice. The girls will be prepared for their next lesson and I am getting myself together musically as well. It's all under control. Now we have to go. We have a lot of activities to get to today."

"Ok . . . I'm glad to hear that. Let me just say a quick hello to Eve?"

Mama walks outside while Eve tells Papa about her makeover her job and the play she's reading. Mama is only half dressed.

She's wearing a big holey t-shirt that barely covers her butt and loose underwear.

"Makeda. It's going to be a hot one today." She says stretching upward like a cat in the cabin doorway.

"Are you gonna put on some clothes?" I ask.

Mama turns and raises her left eyebrow. "Are you?"

I look down and realize that I'm only wearing a pair of shorts and my sports bra. But my chest is so flat that I barely need it. I giggle. Outside the front door there's nothing but the van staring back at us and then layers and layers of trees. The next cabin is about a mile down the road and hidden off a dirt path like ours.

"HELLO! IS THERE ANYBODY OUT THERE?" I scream into the trees. Silence.

"See?" Mama says laughing. "This is the most private place on earth. It's like no one else matters. Except the three of us. Who needs clothes?" And with that she throws off her shirt and walks back inside fully topless.

Exploring

By "a lot of activities to do today" Mama means knitting and watching movies. She doesn't say a word about practicing piano and her violin stays untouched in her room. Instead she throws the pancake dishes on top of the growing pile in the sink and then sets herself up on the floor surrounded by yarn and begins knitting furiously. Eve has convinced her to put on a robe.

"We're not nudists. I'm not coming down the ladder unless you put something on." She'd said peering down into the main room after hanging up with Papa.

"Ok. Ok. But you should try being naked sometime. It's freeing."

"I'm naked when I shower. That's enough for me."

Now we lounge around. Our legs and arms flung all over the main room. Eve on the chair. Me on the love seat and Mama on the floor. We watch *Bridget Jones's Diary* on Netflix and then the sequel. About halfway through the second movie Mama joins me on the love seat and falls asleep.

Outside the cabin the sun beats down. It's almost the end of July and the temperatures get as high as 85 degrees. Even though the windows are open and two big fans whir in our faces I start to sweat. It's a perfect day to go tubing on the river or sunbathe on the big rocks at Boulder Creek like Mama promised we'd do. My legs are pinned under Mama's. They start to go numb and I shift slowly hoping not to disturb her.

"Pssst!" I wave my hand at Eve who is playing some game on her phone. "Want to go explore? I'm bored."

"Not really. It looks even hotter out there."

"Do you think Mama will take us tubing later?"

"Maybe. But for now let's just chill. She'll wake up soon. Then we can ask."

I look at Mama. She's slumped down even further on the love seat. Her legs curled up to her chin like a baby. She snores. And snores. And snores. Like she hasn't slept for days.

"That could take forever." I say getting up. "I'm going to go explore around the woods in the cabin."

"Don't go too far." Eve yells.

But I am already out the door.

A Girlhood Is a Terrible-Wonderful Time

Especially when you're in the mountains. Near the woodpile by the side of the cabin I find a long thick stick. I shake off a few leaves and bugs and plant it firmly against the moist ground and then lean on it. *This is my day. My walking stick.* I set out down the dirt road and then veer off to the right into a thicket of spruce and aspen trees. I walk until I can only see the very top of the cabin through it all. Until I am surrounded by new noises and smells. Then I stop.

"THIS IS MY MOUNTAIN." I scream into the air around me.

I fall to the ground and body-kiss the damp perfumed earth. A girlhood is a terrible-wonderful time. It makes me squirm with impatience. It makes me smash strange berries between my fingers till they are sticky with dirt and juice. It makes me turn over rocks. Pull wriggling earthworms from underneath. Watch them try and burrow back into dark. I think about Lena. Doing back handspring after back handspring at camp. Trying to be the best. How much I miss her. And her letters. I think about Huck. How far away I am from him. I feel a hot glow in my chest. An ache. I think about Mama holding the phone away from her like something venomous. About Papa. Trying trying. But never making her happy these days. I think about my birth mother. *What makes her happy? Who loves her?* A girlhood is a terrible-wonderful time. I look up. A branch of a nearby tree sits low and inviting. *Where can it take me?*

I leave my stick and stand up. I scrape every angle of my knees trying to climb the tree as high as I can. I am so tall. I open my mouth but before I can test my voice against the clear air the Georgia Belles appear on the branch below me. They look like two blackbirds but they sing with familiar and clear tones.

Fly fly fly

Climb on climb on

Into a song

Baby girl baby bird

Something's not right

Fly fly fly

Till you're back in sight

On the ground or in the sky

You need to stay close

Stay close

Stay

Close to us

I have not seen them since the slap. Since I told them I didn't need their help. But they only stay now for a few seconds. They sing the thoughts right out of my head and then dive and swoop away into the path below. I don't have to tell them to wait. When I climb back down they are there. Their voices darting in and out of brush ahead. So I follow the song. The one that's aching. Until I am back at the cabin. Where Eve sits outside while inside Mama grabs all the pots and pans from the sink and throws them out the window. One by one.

"NO ONE APPRECIATES ME!" She yells. "I DO EVERYTHING AROUND HERE. I AM NOT YOUR MAID. I AM NOT YOUR SERVANT. THIS PLACE IS A MESS. YOU DON'T DESERVE ALL THESE CLOTHES. I NEVER HAD THIS MANY NEW CLOTHES WHEN I WAS YOUR AGE. I WILL RETURN ALL OF IT YOU UNGRATEFUL . . ."

"What happened?" I pant.

Eve takes the headphones out of her ears. "No idea. She woke up and then just started yelling. I told her I'd do the dishes but it's like she didn't hear me. I'd wait out here if I were you. She's acting like a total maniac."

I sit next to Eve. She lets me lean my head on her shoulders. We watch the sun set. When the stars come out we hear Mama slam the door to her room. Then it is quiet. We spend the rest of the night in our loft. I can't get the Georgia Belles' song out of my head. *Stay close. Stay close.* I squeeze my eyes shut and wish for a new day.

Fun Fun Fun

We never make it tubing. We never finish our knitting projects. Or any of the other fun fun fun things Mama said we'd do on this trip. The next day Eve and I collect the pots and pans from the yard and scrub them clean in the kitchen. Eve washes and I dry and we don't talk at all. We just get into a rhythm and before we know it the whole cabin is spotless. We even refold all the clothes Mama bought us and put them neatly back into the shopping bags. So they will be easy to return. Around noon Mama emerges from her room. We stand by the sink waiting for her to notice the clean cabin. She doesn't even look at us. Instead she sits on the love seat and turns on the TV.

"Do you want to go for a hike?" I ask. Even though Eve is pinching my arm. Hoping I'll stay quiet.

"What? No." Mama says arranging herself back into a fetal position. "I'm very tired girls. My head is killing me. I just need to rest."

"Here." I run to the cabinet and grab a tall glass. I fill it with cold water. Then I rush to the bathroom and grab a bottle of aspirin. I bring it to Mama and watch her drink a couple pills down. “Maybe that will help.” I say.

Mama looks at me. Her eyes all glassy with tears. “You’re mine. My baby girl.” She says finally. “Remember that Makeda. I was the first one who held you. The day we adopted you. I’m your mother. The one who takes care of you. Nobody else.”

She’s not making any sense. *I’m taking care of you. I have two mothers. You both held me.* I want to say but instead I look up at Eve who is still standing by the sink. As if her feet are glued to the floor. She shrugs and mouths to me: “Just leave her alone?” But I can tell she’s confused as well.

“I know. I love you too.” I say back to Mama who has closed her eyes. “Get some sleep so later tonight we can have more fun fun fun! Just like you said.”

“Sure. Sure. You girls go. Have fun. Take the shuttle into town if you want. There’s money in my purse. I’ll see you later.”

So Eve and I tiptoe out of the cabin. And into the hot hot midday sun.

Independent Women

Eve and I stand outside for about an hour trying to decide what to do. I tell her we should ask Papa to come home early after all. She tells me that we just need to stay out of Mama's way. The sun slices through the trees. The sky streaked with light clouds. The hairs on my neck won't lie flat. I keep peeking in the cabin door to make sure Mama is still on the love seat. She hasn't moved at all.

"Listen." Eve sighs and looks at the time on her phone. "This is not helping. Us just standing here. It's already 1pm. Let's go try to enjoy this day. We can take the shuttle into downtown and get ice cream and walk around. Then we'll come home in a couple of hours and check on her. If she doesn't snap out of it then we can call Papa."

"But what if she's not ok?" *Stay close. Stay close.*

"Keda! She's fine. We're fine. You heard her. She just needs to rest. I can't believe she dragged us all the way out here just to be like she is at home. But here we are. Let's be independent or whatever. Just like she's always telling us to."

Eve calls the shuttle and in no time at all we arrive downtown. We have a wad of cash from Mama's purse and even though we know we could treat ourselves. We don't go overboard.

"Want to get manicures?" Eve points to a fancy salon. "Nobody is here to tell us we can't."

"No." I look down at my stubby raw nails. "No thanks."

"Yeah. I guess we don't need to give Mama a reason to throw any more pots right?"

"Right." I say.

"That was supposed to be a joke."

"Haha! SO funny."

We keep walking. Eve keeps checking the time on her phone. I find new skin around my fingernails and chew on it. We get soft serve and then sit on a bench. The mall buzzes around us like a well-choreographed dance. We watch people walk by. Mothers with their daughters. Groups of giggling friends. Wobbling toddlers. A pack of skaters. A group of senior citizens speed-walking the perimeter. At some point I stop seeing faces and everything melts together. I get dizzy and toss my cone which feels too sweet to eat somehow.

"We should go back." I say. After only an hour.

"I know."

"Now." I say.

Even the Aspen Trees

Are hushed. Their gray trunks leaning toward the sagging cabin in stiff warning. The afternoon sun so bright it cuts my eyes and turns Eve's cheeks raw. Thirty minutes later we jump out of the shuttle and make our way up the front path. Behind us we hear the bus's wheels grinding the gravel as it turns and then speeds away. I grab Eve's limp hand. She wiggles it free. We stand at the slightly open door listening. Listening.

"Go in." I whisper.

"Stay here." She says.

But I follow her through the door.

Inside the light hits the stale air. I watch thousands of delicate dust particles float to the floor.

"She's not in her room." Eve gasps as she looks around.

"She left us?" I say.

"KEDA! She's here!" Eve yells at me through my panic.

In the coat closet. On top of all our shoes. We find Mama. Her lips bluing. She is slumped into the dark corner. Cedar smell. Dust dust dust falling onto her messy braid. Her hands tangled in her knitting.

"Pills. A bunch of pills. Aspirin. Vicodin. Xanax. I dunno! Pills. Wine." I hear Eve on the cabin phone with 911.

And then Mama mumbles: "Sorry. I tried."

And all I can think is: *Stay. Stay. Don't leave me.* But I am afraid to go to her. To move. So instead I give her a big frozen smile and stand like this until the ambulance comes.

Suicide (noun)

The decision to end one's own life.

In the hospital waiting room I look up the word on Eve's phone. Eve is sitting next to me. Crying. And Aunt Sarah is holding her.

"It's not your fault." I hear Aunt Sarah say. "Our dad. Your grandpa. He had really bad depressions too. You girls did the right thing."

It's not your fault. These are the same words the social worker had said to us a few hours before. Eve and I rode in the ambulance and Eve called Aunt Sarah on the drive to the hospital. When we arrived Eve and I had to wait in a small room while they rolled Mama away to have her stomach pumped. We had to be interviewed together and then separately by the social worker. He asked us a bunch of questions. *Did we have food? Where was our dad? Had Mama tried to hurt us? How long had we been at the cabin? Had she tried to hurt herself before?* It went on and on. I was so tired. And then. When it was over. Aunt Sarah was there.

I look at the word on the computer screen now. I think about Mama's limp head. Bowed over her chest. About all the tubes and beeping things she'd been hooked up to in the ambulance. How weak and pale she was. How she couldn't even look at us. Holding her hands. Sitting right next to her. She'd just turned her head away. Away from us. Her own daughters.

"It's not your fault. You did the right thing calling 911. Calling me. Your mom just needs time to heal." I hear Aunt Sarah say again.

But did we? I have a terrible pain in my gut. Like meat grinding. *Do the right thing? Did I?* All summer long I was alone in the house with Mama. All summer long. So worried. All summer long sneaking out of bed to watch her cry. Listen for her breathing. All summer long. So angry. Dreaming of another mother. All summer trying to soak up her sadness.

I love. I hurt. I want. I love. I hurt. I want. All summer like this. Dreaming of another life. *Silly girl.* The Georgia Belles whispersing in my ear. *That's what the blues are all about.*

Aunt Sarah

Is Mama's older sister. By two years. She works as a veterinarian in Denver Colorado which is about an hour away from Boulder. Her house is one of my favorite places to visit. It's full of colorful glass vases. Wind chimes and bird feeders. And dogs. And rabbits. And fish. And once even a monkey named Ezra.

But today it is hard to be here. It's hard to face the sunlight streaming through Aunt Sarah's kitchen. It's hard to care about the sugary French toast Aunt Sarah has prepared for us. Even the ten fluffy baby bunnies Aunt Sarah is raising in a hutch on her back porch cannot undo the events of yesterday.

Outside in my pjs after breakfast I pick up a small white bunny named Daisy. I hold her to my pounding chest and bury my face in the fur at the back of her neck. But I cannot unsee Mama turning away from us. Mama's limp hand waving away Papa's worried face on Aunt Sarah's phone once we got to see her again in her hospital room. The *beep beep beep* and *whir whir whir* of machines keeping people alive and stable.

At some point yesterday. After the social worker interviewed us. After Mama's stomach was pumped and she was tucked away in her room in the psych ward. After Aunt Sarah filled out all the paperwork while Eve and I tried to eat grilled cheeses in the cafeteria. We were released into Aunt Sarah's care until Papa could make it back to the States. Aunt Sarah drove us home in her Jeep and made up an air mattress for us in her home office. We both arranged ourselves on the mattress to try and sleep. Eve played Candy Crush or Cookie Smash or some stupid game until her phone died. Then we both just lay there. In the dark. Trying not to hear Aunt Sarah on the phone with Papa. With the hospital.

"Eve?" I said after a long while.

"Yeah?"

"Do you think Mama will ever look at us again?"

"I dunno Keda. I don't know anything anymore. What she did was really selfish."

And I didn't know what to say then. And soon Eve started to snore. But I was still awake. So I jammed my eyes shut. Over and over again. Hoping that the Georgia Belles would be in the room to comfort me when I opened them. But they never showed up. And the only songs in my head last night were crashing ones. Metal and screeching and noise.

"Where are they when I need them the most?" I whisper in Daisy's ear now. And Daisy jumps out of my arms and back into her cage where she is safe.

Reunion

Mama goes into the Boulder hospital on Sunday night and by Tuesday morning Papa arrives with his cello and all his bags. I've never seen him so pale. He is as white as computer paper. He has dark circles and little wrinkles around his eyes. We are in the hospital waiting room. It's 11am and Aunt Sarah is behind us checking in. We spent most of Monday at the hospital and Mama has been silent each time we visit her room. But Aunt Sarah just talks to her as if she's talking back. And I hold Mama's hand. Eve mostly stands in the corner. I think she might really hate Mama.

But now Papa is here too. "My girls—" He starts to say but before Papa can finish his greeting we are both in his arms. He smells like airplane food and sweat but we don't care. We hug him tight and he doesn't let go until Aunt Sarah's voice breaks in.

"Daniel. I'm sorry. The front desk needs some information from you."

"Of course." Papa says giving Aunt Sarah a quick hug. "Thank you."

Aunt Sarah and Eve sit back down but I follow Papa to the front desk. I stand next to him as he confirms insurance information and signs a bunch of documents. His bushy eyebrows furrow in concentration and in between documents he bites the end of the pen cap between his teeth. When he's finished he looks down at me and smiles.

"I think you've gotten taller since I left little scoop!"

"Yeah right. It hasn't been that long."

"Still. You look taller. And wiser."

"Well. I'm eleven and a half now."

Papa laughs and pulls me in for another hug. "That you are my love." He says. "I'm so sorry these months have been so rough. Thank you for being a big girl."

"Is Mama getting out today? Now that you're here?"

"I don't know yet. I have to speak with the psychiatrist. We'll see. The most important thing is that she is safe. And that you and your sister are safe."

"Ok." I say. "But she's going to be ok right? She's going to come home?"

"Let's just take it one day at a time. Today I'm here. So I can get all the information and we'll see. I know this is hard."

Papa and I join Eve and Aunt Sarah on the stiff blue couches. We wait for another twenty minutes and finally it's time.

"Girls." Aunt Sarah starts. "Let's let your dad go in first. So he can get a little time with your mom."

"She's not going to speak to you you know." Eve blurts. "She's basically mute now. She doesn't even want to be alive. I think she made that very clear."

"Eve." Aunt Sarah whispers. "Stop. We're all worried."

"I'm not worried! I'm glad she's stopped talking. It's always all about her. Finally. We can hear ourselves think."

"SHUT UP!" I yell. "Just shut up Eve."

"Eve." Papa begins. "I'm so sorry this happened. It must have been so scary."

"Well. You're not the one that should be apologizing. I'm fine. She's the mental case."

Papa sighs and gives Aunt Sarah a pained look.

"Ok. Let's go get some fresh air. Then we can join your dad in your mom's room."

I watch Papa head through a pair of swinging doors. I want to run after him. I want to jump on his back like I used to when I was little. I want to run into that room with him and see Mama smiling. Mama holding her arms out to all of us. Like she's been waiting for this. A reunion. But instead I follow Eve and Aunt Sarah outside where it spits rain and the clouds are gray and heavy.

Psychiatric Evaluation (noun)

The evaluation of a person's mental social and psychological health.

Mama can't leave the psych unit of the hospital until she has completed her 72-hour psychiatric hold. "When someone tries to hurt themselves. It's a very serious matter. And we have to keep them here for three days. Even if they don't want to be here." A doctor in green scrubs explains to us. We are all crowded into Mama's room. She's propped up by three pillows but her head is turned away from us.

"I told them I'm fine now. This is like prison." Mama says to no one in particular.

LOOK AT US. TALK TO US. I want to yell. I hold Papa's hand instead. It shakes and I grip tighter. Everything about the room we are in is too bright. Fluorescent lights line the ceiling in neat rows. There is a blinding glare bouncing off of the doctor's white white teeth as she explains what will happen next.

"So. Your mother is going to stay here for a little longer. We've already done an initial evaluation. But given that this isn't her first bad depression. And after speaking with some of your mother's old therapists. We need to dive a little deep. And this will help us understand what's going on here so she's safe and healthy."

"How much longer is 'a little longer'?" Eve asks.

"Well. It's hard to say exactly. We can't legally hold her past tomorrow. But now that your dad's here he and your mom might want to talk about extending care. We need to figure out why your mother is feeling this way. And then we'll need to come up with a plan for treatment. So this doesn't happen again."

"She's sad. Depressed. How hard can it be to figure out what's happening?" Eve says.

"Eve." Aunt Sarah begins. "It's not that simple. Remember we talked about this. Let the doctor talk."

"Well. Eve. You're right. But when someone is this sad. So sad they want to end their life it can be more than just depression. And that's what we want to make sure we find out. Ok? You both have been very brave and patient. Your mom's just going to need some time to heal."

We are standing there talking about Mama like she's a ghost. Like she can't hear us. And I don't want her to be hurting anymore. She's been hurting all summer and all I've done is watch her. Ignore her. Dream about being somewhere else. I don't realize I am crying until Papa pulls a handkerchief from his pocket and starts wiping my nose.

“Now.” The doctor says. “Do you have any other questions before I leave you to visit a little longer?”

I have so many questions but I feel Papa loosen his grip. “No. Thank you.” He says. “I think that’s good for now.”

And then we are alone. In the quiet bright room. And Mama keeps her arms crossed. And Eve stares out the window. And Aunt Sarah starts fussing with the TV volume. And Papa sits on the end of the bed. And I feel that stupid smile growing on my face. The one I can’t stop when I’m feeling scared. So I bite my tongue. Hard. Till I taste blood. Then I bury my nose in Papa’s handkerchief. And blow.

Blessings

When we return from the hospital that afternoon (without Mama) Papa is so exhausted he takes a shower and falls asleep until dinner. At 7pm Aunt Sarah orders Thai food and makes us sit down together even though nobody feels much like talking or eating.

"Well. This won't do." She says after a long silence. "I know we are all worried about your mom but the universe has provided us with many blessings as well. She's safe. And I am so glad to have my two nieces and brother-in-law staying with me. And it's not even Christmas!"

"Oh man. You sound just like Mama." Eve says. "All that universe talk."

"Well. Where do you think she got it from?" Aunt Sarah says. Her eyes twinkling.

"And at least we are not still in that cabin. Alone." I shudder at the thought.

"That's right." Papa chimes in. "I am so glad you acted quickly and made the call to 911 Eve. It's a blessing you were able to get through to help so quickly. Even on the mountain."

"Are you serious?" Eve's eyes are wide and wild. "Oh so you

mean like counting it a blessing that you left us in the first place Papa? That you moved us away from our friends and then ditched us for weeks with a crazy person who basically kidnapped us in the middle of the night and brought us to some cabin in the woods? Yeah. I feel super blessed. I've for sure lost my job at this point. And now we're stuck here. In this zoo. This house smells like a zoo. It's disgusting."

"Eve!"

"It's ok Daniel." Aunt Sarah says. "She's just upset. She's allowed to be upset."

"Oh I am? Thanks. Thanks for stating the obvious. I hate all of you." And with that Eve kicks back her chair and leaves the table.

"EVE!" Papa bellows after her. "Get back here right now. You will not disrespect your aunt like that. Unbelievable." Papa gets up and chases after Eve.

"How about a movie?" Aunt Sarah says to me as she starts clearing the table. Papa and Eve continue to yell at each other.

"Sure." I say. Even though part of me wants to follow Eve. To fling the dishes off the table and watch them shatter on the floor. I should have been paying more attention. Maybe then we wouldn't be here. *It's my fault. It's my fault. It's my fault.* An ugly little voice sings in my head.

It's a Hard-Knock Life

We decide on the musical *Annie.* The version from the 1980s. "I grew up watching this movie you know?" Aunt Sarah says settling in next to me on the couch.

"I know." I say. "This is one of Mama's favorites."

In the kitchen Papa is on the phone. At least he and Eve have stopped screaming at each other. Between musical numbers I hear him sighing scribbling and whisper-talking in the kitchen as he makes plans for Mama's release.

Halfway through the movie Eve sulks in. "I'm glad you're watching this version." She says pointing at the TV. "The more recent version is trash."

"Is it?" Aunt Sarah asks. "I haven't seen that one."

"Yeah. I mean it's ok. It's more diverse. It stars that girl whose name is hard to say. It's something like Que-van-nisha. She plays Annie. But I dunno. Don't you think Annie just makes more sense as a redhead?"

It's like I'm not even in the room the way Eve says this. Casually. *That girl whose name is hard to say.*

"Her name is Quvenzhané Wallis." I snap. My lips quivering. "And she was nominated for an Academy Award."

"Oh right. Well whatever." Eve continues. Perching like a parrot on the arm of the couch. "Not for this movie though."

"It's not whatever! That's really rude." I say.

"What's the big deal Keda? You agree with me. You like the old version of *Annie* better too."

I stand up and let the popcorn bowl that is in my lap fall.

"Keda!" Aunt Sarah startles as the bowl crashes on the tile.

But I ignore her. I am in Eve's face now. "That's not the point. Why can't you just say her name right? You say my name right. It's not hard. And what. You don't think I could play Annie?"

"Come on Keda. Don't get so upset. Of course you could. That's not what I said—"

"That IS what you said. And it's mean!"

"Keda. Calm down. You're overreacting. It's not mean. I just think that casting remakes of old movies is hard. Like. I just can't all of a sudden FORGET what the original Annie looked like."

"That's stupid." I am yelling now. "Why not?"

"You know you're being a real pain in the ass." Eve says then.

"Girls!" Aunt Sarah tries to step in. "Enough ok?"

But I keep my body planted in front of Eve's. "WELL I GET TO BE ANGRY TOO!" I yell at the top of my lungs. "YOU'RE NOT THE ONLY ONE. YOU DON'T CARE ABOUT ME AT

ALL DO YOU? YOU THINK I'M A BABY BUT I'M NOT. YOU DON'T CARE ABOUT MAMA AND YOU HAVE BEEN A TOTAL WITCH TO ME THIS WHOLE TIME. YOU DON'T CARE ABOUT ANYONE BUT YOURSELF AND I AM SICK OF IT."

"Let's take a time-out shall we?" Aunt Sarah says. Pausing the movie.

Papa comes into the room now with his hand over the phone. "What is it now?!" He hisses. "Do we have a problem?"

"Are you going to tell him what you said?" I lower my voice but point my finger at Eve's face.

Eve looks at me and then at Aunt Sarah whose eyes fall to the floor. "Aunt Sarah. You agree with me right? I didn't say anything wrong."

"Well." Aunt Sarah starts. "Maybe you could have remembered that actress's name. But this is between you and your sister. I'm not getting involved. You guys have to make your own peace. Solve your own conflicts."

Eve rolls her eyes then. And I know she's thinking Aunt Sarah sounds just like Mama. But instead of apologizing Eve turns back to Papa. "No. There's no problem. Keda's throwing a tantrum because she apparently can't hear right. It's fine. Just sister stuff."

"YOU ARE NOT MY SISTER. YOU ARE AN IGNORANT MONSTER." I scream in Eve's stupid lying face.

And with that. I stomp out of the room and flop onto the air mattress Eve and I share. Aunt Sarah's home office is dark except for the fluorescent light flickering around from the fish tank. I bury my face in my pillow and scream and scream. And it feels good. To let all my rage go. It feels like I'm yelling at Eve and Katy and Alma and everyone who has made my life miserable since we moved. When I finally stop. There are voices in the room with me. Shadows.

You can't stop the rain

You can't stop her pain

When it rains it pours

That's the weather baby girl

That's just the weather

You can't stop the pain

Let it rain let it rain

You can't control the wind

She blows and blows

Ain't a storm

You can stop

Except your own

Let it pour

Let it pour

And let go

"Where have you been?" I hiccup. The Georgia Belles hop from one fluorescent flicker to the next. But they just keep singing. *Let it pour. Let it pour.* So I let the tears fall. I cry for Lena. For the old Eve. For Mama. And I sing along with them until I am calm.

"Little scoop? Are you awake?" Papa's voice calls from the doorway an hour or so later. I squeeze my eyes shut and let out a soft snore. Papa leans over to kiss me on the forehead. "Eve's going to sleep on the couch." He whispers. Tucking the blankets around me. And then. As if he knows I'm fake-sleeping he says into my ear: "You can be anything you want in this world little scoop. Anything."

But I know that. It's Eve who doesn't seem to think so.

Small

By 3pm the next day Mama is released from the hospital. And by 7pm we are all on a plane headed home.

"You can have the window." Eve offers. Trying to make up for our fight. I squeeze past her without a word. "Fine. Be that way." She says settling into the middle seat. She's wearing a black hoodie. She puts on her headphones and pulls the hood over her eyes. She's snoring before we even take off.

Mama and Papa are in the row in front of us. Mama had at least smiled weakly at me and Eve when she and Papa made it back to Aunt Sarah's from the hospital earlier that afternoon. But we didn't get much time before we were loading up all our things into Aunt Sarah's Jeep and racing to the airport.

"I'll be out to visit you in a couple months. When I drive your van back." Aunt Sarah had said. Hugging Mama close at the curb. "You'll have it in no time."

"In one piece." Mama had joked weakly.

"Yeah. Yeah." Aunt Sarah laughed. "I'll try."

Then Aunt Sarah had kissed us all and hopped into her Jeep.

"Let's go before we miss our plane!" Papa said as we watched Aunt Sarah speed away. "I was on the phone all night making these arrangements. Let's just get home so we can get back to normal."

But nothing is normal. Mama looks like a ghost. Eve is acting like a stranger. And Papa is so worried and exhausted he can barely function.

Now. The plane climbs higher and higher. I watch the white circus tent that is the Denver airport grow smaller and smaller. Then we hit the clouds and all I can see is a foggy gray. I don't like it when I can't see the ground. When I don't know where I am or what's below. The plane shakes and dips a little as we climb over the mountains. I close my eyes and try to feel happy that we are all going home. But as the turbulence continues all I can feel is my gut flipping. *What if she tries again and I am not there to stop her? Who will be my mother then? What if we are never the same?*

I hear a ding. The captain has leveled out the plane and turned off the seatbelt sign. No more bumps. I look down. The clouds are now distant streaks below. And the land looks like it has been squashed flat with a hammer. It looks like a patchwork of different-color animal skins and hides. It looks like a bunch of wounds sewn together with thick black thread. I feel like a tiny rock. A shard of sea glass. All worn down to a small grain of useless sand. I do not feel like a girl or a young woman or a sister or a daughter. If it wasn't for Eve snoring next to me. I wouldn't know what or who I was.

Part III: FALL

Labor Day Weekend

Eve and I are not speaking. It's been a month since we fought at Aunt Sarah's and the house is cemetery quiet. Papa tries to get us to make up.

"Little scoop! Big scoop! What's this about? Don't you think we've had enough drama for one summer?" He says on Friday morning as Eve and I do silent dances around each other in the kitchen.

But this just makes Eve explode. "AND WHOSE FAULT IS THAT?" She yells in Papa's face before storming off to the sunroom to eat her oatmeal and read an enormous volume of Shakespeare's plays she's been burying herself in since we got back.

"WELL I'M HERE NOW OK?" Papa yells back. "You need to adjust your attitude young lady! We're all doing our best." He sits at the table. Crunches on his toast and gulps his coffee down in two swallows. "You girls are killing me." He says to me before getting up to gather his scores and cello. "I just have one more rehearsal this morning and then we can spend the holiday weekend together. This has got to end. You cannot be fighting like this when Mama gets back next week."

Even though we all came home together from Boulder Mama left again only a few days after we returned. She voluntarily checked herself into a recovery clinic in Taos.

"What's Mama recovering from?" I keep asking Papa. "I thought she was doing better?"

"She is. She is. But it's complicated. She'll tell you herself when she's back. You just need to trust that she's doing this to be healthy."

I don't understand why Mama can't recover at home. I still wake up at night and check the locks. The doors. A good little soldier. *Can't we help her heal?*

Ain't a storm you can stop. Except your own. The Georgia Belles keep reminding me. But it's hard to let go. Everything is familiar but different. The chickens are bigger. Fireball crows and crows and crows in the morning. Before the light creeps in. Eve and I take turns looking for eggs. Dumping the compost. Homeschool group doesn't start up again for another week or so. So we read more books. I poke around the yard for treasure. I sing made-up songs. Eve memorizes all of *Hamilton*. We practice piano. Each morning I pick out my TWA that's more like a full-on Afro these days. I stuff the messy edges into a headband and try to pat it down. Papa drives us to the grocery store. We shop in silence. The Sandias glow pinker than ever at sunset.

And Mama recovers. She does not write or email. She does

not call. And even though Papa has circled September 6th in red pen on the fridge calendar. I am starting to believe she may never come home. That maybe she's across the world. Playing concerts in her red sequined dress. That somewhere on a stage she bows and bows and bows. And people clap and clap and clap. And her playing is so beautiful. So clear. Nobody can tell. That she's left us all behind.

Mother (noun)

At the library on Saturday I slip away from Papa and Eve. I copy down the definition in my songbook:

1. A woman who is a parent
2. ORIGIN / BEARER OF LIFE
3. One who displays a maternal softness or attentiveness

Then I write the beginning of a new song:

A mother is a puzzle
A face that is mine
And not mine
A mother hurts
Be your own origin

When I get home I call Lena. But nobody picks up and I don't leave a message. I hop on the computer and check our blog.

But even though Lena promised she'd write when she got back from camp in August. There's nothing new from her. I know I should write her. About everything that has happened. But I can't. Not yet.

A Gloomy Sunday

Turns into a gloomy Labor Day Monday. Papa takes us to Target to get "back to school supplies" but public schools started two weeks before and the supplies have been picked over. All that appears to be left are red and blue folders and stacks and stacks of lined paper and some packs of pencils with bananas all over them.

"We should have come here weeks ago like normal kids!" Eve whines at Papa as we pick through the leftovers. "All the good stuff is gone."

"Well that's not true!" Papa says with a forced smile. "You just have to dig a little."

"Yeah right. We'd have to dig to another Target to find anything." I add. "All of this is the worst stuff. The stuff nobody wants."

"Come on girls. Give me a break. Next year we'll get here earlier ok?"

"Ok." Eve says.

"Fine." I say.

But neither of us can get rid of our sour faces. It feels like we are always getting the leftovers.

I dig through a pile of plain black composition notebooks. But don't find any neon ones hiding. Eve throws a white three-ring binder in the cart and then grabs a pack of yellow highlighters.

"That's all I really need. So I can keep my script organized and learn my lines." She says. Wandering in the direction of the shoe department.

As a compromise. For being told that neither she nor I would be going back to El Rio. That we were going to "give the home-school thing a fair shot but with more structure and help." Papa let Eve enroll in an after-school theater group at the Downtown Theater Association. Eve's hoping to get the role of Katherina in this fall's youth production of *The Taming of the Shrew.* If we were speaking I'd tell her that role is perfect for her. Since she's so grumpy and mean all the time. But I keep my mouth shut. I'm relieved to not be going back to El Rio. Papa hired a tutor to come work on math and science with us twice a week and we'll both be taking some online courses as well as continuing to attend homeschool group.

When we get home from shopping. I call Lena again. Her mom never has her phone on her. The phone rings and rings and rings. Then I get sent to her mom's voice mail.

"It's Labor Day weekend." Papa reminds me as I hand back his phone. "She's probably out with her family. I'm sure she'll call you back."

I'm not. I've called her five times since being home. I'm starting to think maybe she forgot about me.

"Why aren't we out? With our family I mean?" I ask.

"We just went out."

"You know what I mean."

Papa takes off his glasses and rubs the bridge of his nose. Then he smiles at me and pats the space beside him on the couch where he is seated with his laptop and headphones. "I know. But Mama's home tomorrow. And we're going to spend some time together. With her. I promise. Plus. Once I finish this work I'll make us turkey burgers. How does that sound?"

"Turkey burgers are gross."

"Well. I also got fries. Will you eat fries at least?"

"Maybe." I say scooting off the couch. "Probably."

Papa sighs and then puts his headphones back on. I head down the hall. I stop by Eve's room. The door is open. Eve is standing in front of her closet mirror reading Katherina's lines dramatically from her huge Shakespeare book.

"If I be waspish best beware my sting!" Eve says in a shrill and exaggerated tone. "If I BE waspish BEST beware my STING!" She says again. This time accenting different syllables.

Before I can stop myself I laugh out loud.

Eve turns sharply. "What are you laughing at!"

"You. That was funny."

"Well your face is funny." And she slams her door in my face.

"WAY TO TAKE A COMPLIMENT!" I yell through the closed door. "THAT'S WHY I'M NOT TALKING TO YOU."

"WELL YOU JUST DID." Eve yells back.

I pound her door with my fists two times and then head into my own room. I take the picture of the two of us on my dresser and shove it into the back of my closet. *Who needs her? The shrew.* I spend the rest of the afternoon listening to Billie Holiday's "Gloomy Sunday." Over and over and over. Outside the sun shines and shines and shines. I get up and close my curtains. I don't think about Mama. Or Eve. Or Papa. I close my eyes and let Billie tell me all about my feelings.

Bad Jokes

The next day we drive three hours north to pick up Mama from her clinic in Taos. Eve sits in the front with Papa and I sit behind her in the back seat of Papa's Volvo. We wind our way into the jagged hills and then onto thin mountain roads that make me dizzy and out of breath with their height.

For the first hour we listen to Papa tell bad jokes. "What did the red light say to the green light? . . . Don't look! I'm changing! What do you get when you drop a piano down a mine shaft? . . . A flat minor. Why did Adele cross the road? . . . To say hello to the other side. What's the difference between a viola and an onion? . . . Nobody cries when you cut up a viola."

I smile at that one. And from the front seat I hear Eve snort.

"Aha!" Papa shouts. "You DO still know how to have some fun."

I get what he's trying to do. Lighten the mood. Eve didn't even want to come with us. But Papa wouldn't let her stay home. And I want to see Mama. With my own eyes. *What if she's still not better?* My stomach flips with the thought and then growls with hunger since I wasn't able to keep my breakfast down. None of us really know what to expect when we get there. All Papa tells us is that we're going to meet with Mama and her therapist for a family counseling session. And then afterward we can check her out of the clinic and bring her home.

"Hey. Here's a cool joke." Eve starts. "One out of every four people is suffering from some mental imbalance. Look around at three people you know. If they're ok. Then YOU'RE THE CRAZY ONE."

Papa doesn't laugh.

And neither do I. "I don't get it."

"Oh come on. It's funny because—"

"That's enough." Papa says with ice in his voice. "Cut it out Eve. Mental illness is nothing to joke about. You should know that. I don't want to hear any of that EVER again. Have some empathy why don't you!"

Eve slams her body back in her seat and puts her headphones on. So Papa turns on Beethoven's Fifth Symphony and maxes out the speaker volume. We drive the rest of the way like this. Eve's headphones blaring. The Volvo's sound system blaring back. By the time we get to the clinic my ears ring and ring and ring with noise.

Brightree Clinic and Retreat

Mama looks smaller. Like she's lost weight. I thought maybe she'd be in a white paper gown like at the hospital but she is wearing her own clothes. A pair of jeans and a black and white striped t-shirt that hangs off of her. Her hair is pulled back into one long braid. She smiles at us when we walk into Dr. Deb's office. Then she bites her bottom lip. Her eyes filling with moisture. My heart pounds. *Why is she still crying? Shouldn't she be feeling better? What kind of stupid clinic is this!* But before I lose it Mama is hugging me. And then Papa. And she is also laughing. "I missed you." She motions for Eve to join us but Eve just says "hi" and then hovers in the doorway. She looks small too. Standing alone. Her ponytail escaping her black hoodie. Biting her bottom lip. Just like Mama does.

Dr. Deb's office is not really an office so much as a big room decorated like a beach house. Which is funny. Because we are in the high desert. No water in sight for miles. The walls are painted an eggshell blue. And photos of boats and driftwood and oceans hang on them. Besides a desk and chair in the far corner there are no other real pieces of furniture in the room.

“Alright. Let’s make a circle and all have a seat.” Dr. Deb says. Motioning to the middle of the room where an assortment of pillows are spread out. “We like to ground ourselves here. Sitting on the floor helps.”

I pick a big square purple pillow made of velvet. Eve picks a plain black one and sits next to me. She sits so close I can feel her sleeve tickling my arm. *Of course Mama picked the hippie dippie crunchy clinic!* I can almost feel her saying.

“So.” Dr. Deb begins. “Here’s how this is going to work. Your mother has some things to share with you. About what she’s been going through these past months. And then you all will have a chance to speak. Ask any questions. Share thoughts or feelings you may have. I am here simply to support this conversation. And offer any knowledge I may have after treating and getting to know Anna during her time here.”

Mama shifts nervously on her pillow. Papa reaches for her hand. But she doesn’t notice and instead clasps them together. Making a tight fist with her knuckles. “This is harder than I thought.” She says. Glancing at all of us and then looking at Dr. Deb. “I know I put you all through a lot this summer . . . and . . . well. I need you to know that I’m really committed to addressing this. Head-on.”

“What even is THIS?” Eve speaking a full sentence for the

first time since we arrived. "Why can't anybody just give us a clear answer?"

"Eve." Dr. Deb says. "That's a very valid question. Let your mom finish."

"I have a mental illness called bipolar disorder." Mama begins. Looking down at her hands. "Bipolar II. I've sort of known something was not right for many years but I didn't want to admit it. In fact. Dr. Shell my therapist in Baltimore suspected I was bipolar when I was still seeing her. But then I stopped going before we moved. I just didn't want to hear it. I don't like the idea of being a sick person. I thought I could just ignore it. I thought it was normal to have such big feelings all the time. It's part of what makes me an artist! But. As you know. It got really bad this summer."

Mama keeps talking. But I am going through words and definitions in my brain. Trying to remember anything about mental illness or bipolar but I come up blank.

"So." Dr. Deb steps in now. "Bipolar can affect how a person feels acts and thinks. It's an illness of the brain. It affects everyone differently. But there are two general moods that happen to a person with bipolar disorder."

Dr. Deb keeps talking. But it's as if she turns into a robot reading definitions to us out loud. I close my eyes. I am still dizzy with the altitude and this information is making it worse.

Mood 1: Depressed *(adjective)*

"This is when your mother is feeling very low and sad. It's different than regular depression because when she's in this state it's very hard for your mom to stop feeling this way."

Mood 2: Manic *(adjective)*

"This is when your mother feels like everything is great. She might have a ton of energy. Her thoughts race and she has a lot of new ideas and might start projects. Spend money. She can be really happy one moment but also very irritable the next. She can also do things that are dangerous because she may feel like she can do anything."

"Like shredding all your music?" I find myself saying out loud.

Papa looks over at me and raises his eyebrow. Eve shifts even closer to me. Her arm leaning into mine hard. Like she is having a hard time sitting up on her own. Mama rubs her hands together. But looks me right in the eye. "Yes." She says quietly. "I was most likely manic that day. I didn't really think about what I was doing."

Mama is so small. She looks like a little girl. Sitting there. Biting her lip. I know she is telling us something important. But the tips of my ears get hot hot hot. All summer. Me and Mama alone in the house. And *she knew. She knew. She knew something was wrong for years.* My head rings and rings and rings. Dr. Deb's mouth is opening and closing now. And Papa is also talking. But I don't hear them. Eve leans into me like a fallen tree. I lean back into her. We sit there and try to understand that Mama is still Mama. But also. She is a stranger.

"Do you girls have any questions?" Mama's voice breaks through the ringing finally.

I shake my head. My head that feels so light. Like a dried leaf. I might just float away.

"This is not easy. For me. And I'm going to be managing my bipolar for the rest of my life. Taking medication that helps my moods and also making sure I'm going to therapy again. Every week. And exercising. But girls. I just want you two to know. That this is not your fault. It's just the way my brain chemicals work. And it's not always going to be easy. But thanks to my time here I've gained some tools and routines to be healthier."

"Do I have it?" I feel Eve lean back into herself. Her voice cool and smoky like a field right after lightning has struck. "I mean. Is it like cancer? If someone in your family has it can we get it too one day?"

Mama looks at Dr. Deb.

"No. Eve. You don't have it. It is true that genes affect the way our bodies develop. And yes you do share genes with your mom and dad. And sometimes people with bipolar also have a family member who has had it." Dr. Deb confirms. "But Eve. I don't want you to worry. Bipolar is something that shows up later in life. Far from now. And when you know the signs and what to look for it is very treatable and manageable. So as long as you go to the doctor regularly. And take care of yourself. No matter what happens. Even if it turns out that one day you do develop bipolar symptoms. You're going to be just fine. And so is your mom."

But not me? What about me? My head floats.

Eve is sitting up on her own now. No. She is standing up. "This is BS." She says. "I do not think we should be listening to some witchy doctor who doesn't even have any real furniture in her office! What do you even know about us? About our family. You think you know my mom after one stupid month! I've known her my WHOLE LIFE. And she is not sick. She just had a bad summer. We are not sick. This is trash. TRASH!!!!!" With that Eve kicks her pillow and storms out of the office. "I'll be by the car." She yells.

Papa reaches for Mama's hands. This time she sees and lets him take them both in his. "I'll go talk to her." He says. I wind my shoestrings around my fingers.

Dr. Deb says: "I know this is hard. It's going to be a process for everyone."

And I know she's trying to help. But I want to throw my pillow at her. *We. Are. Not. Broken.* My head screams.

Hereditary (adjective)

While Mama and Papa check out in the Brightree lobby. I look up the word on Papa's phone.

Characteristics that are passed or capable of being passed from parent to child through the genes.

When I hit USE IT IN A SENTENCE a recorded voice says: "Blue eyes are hereditary in our family."

Bipolar is hereditary in our family. I repeat in my head. *Freckles are hereditary in our family.* And I can't stop thinking of all the new ways I do and do not belong. Because. As Dr. Deb explained to me after Eve stormed out. "Genes are passed from biological parents to their biological children. So you. You share genes with your birth mother. But not your mom."

And I know I should be positive for Mama. So we can all start the "healing process." But as we head to the car I can't stop thinking a horrible thought: *What traits did I get from my biological mom? How will my body and mind develop as I get older?*

"Are you coming Makeda?"

I am frozen in the parking lot.

"What's wrong?" Mama is holding the car door open for me.

But I can't speak. I am having a hard time breathing. We are so high up. In the mountains. And I feel so small. As if the sky is pressing down on me. Pressing me back into the earth like a seed.

"Come here peach." Mama is saying to me now. Hcr arms wide open. "It's ok. It's ok. Breathe."

I pick up one foot and then the other. And then I am in her arms. Gasping for air. Crying. As Mama smooths my forehead and kisses my cheeks and holds me tight. Like I needed her to hold me all summer long.

Showing

We are home again. I cannot sleep even though I am so tired from my outburst by the car. Mama and Papa went to bed hours ago. But when I peek out my door. I can see Eve's light still on. My chest throbs. She's been in her room since we got back. Since she leaned her whole weight into me at Brightree. And then stood up and left me alone.

"Let's give her some space." Mama had said. "She's angry with me. Let her be angry. I'll talk to her soon." And so on the drive home Eve sat next to me with her headphones on. Staring out the window. Her arms crossed against her chest. And in the front seat. Mama did the same. Except she and Papa listened to NPR on the radio. Eve didn't even notice I was crying.

No. Leave her alone. She doesn't care about you. So I close the door to my room. I build a nest with my blankets. I curl up like a baby bird in the middle of it. I try and fall into a dream but every time I open my eyes I am in my room. Scenes from the long scary summer flashing before my eyes. Around 2am I hear a tapping at my window. Footsteps. Humming. I open my window and the Georgia Belles swarm in. Smelling like the mountains at dusk.

Sun kissed and dusty. But in my room they are smaller than I remember. Their shadows my height or even a little shorter. Their voices still clear and true.

Keda girl Keda girl
Get up get up
The world's a hurt
The world's a storm
Hold on to your own
Keda girl Keda girl
Give give give
Live live live
You gotta make mistakes
To grow grow grow
Let your words go
Let yourself show

And before I know what's good for me. Before I can open my mouth and answer with my anger. I am on my feet. I am across the hall. I am opening Eve's door. I am crawling into bed with her. Where she too is curled like a baby bird. Sobbing.

Inheritance

"I'm scared." Eve says.

"Me too." And it's a small relief to not be patrolling the house or fighting with my blankets or singing/arguing with the Georgia Belles. Eve and I are curled like two yin yang halves in her bed. We are under her blanket. Eve flips on her iPhone flashlight. And then we are our own little planet. I wait for Eve to kick me out or say more but she doesn't. We lie in our silence and just breathe. I imagine that the two of us are floating through space. Nobody knows where we are. Except the stars.

"You still awake?" Eve says after a while.

"Yep."

"Oh. Ok. Well thanks for coming in here. I was kinda losing it I guess."

"Yeah. I know."

"How?"

"Just had a feeling. We're sisters after all."

Eve starts taking in big gulps of air. She's crying again. "So. You don't hate me?" She manages to get out.

"I thought you hated me." And as soon as the words escape

my mouth I feel my shoulders loosen and I unclench my palms. I did not realize I was holding them in tight fists.

"No." Eve says. "I don't hate you. I just. Well I guess right now I'm just mad at myself. I sometimes feel like I'll never be normal. You know?"

Normal. That's a word I look up a lot.

(Adjective)—Common or ordinary: not peculiar

"YOU don't feel normal?" I can't believe it. "But you fit in everywhere! You make friends so easy and you get jobs and you look just like Mama."

"What's that got to do with anything? Looking like Mama?"

Let yourself show. Let yourself show. "I just don't think you know what it feels like. Not to look like anyone. That's all. Where do I fit?"

"You fit here! With us. Your family."

"Sometimes. But then sometimes I don't. Like when we fought at Aunt Sarah's."

Eve sits up now. She wipes her face with the back of her hand. "I know." She says after a long pause. "I'm really sorry. I don't know why I said what I did . . . it was . . ."

"Racist."

"Right. Ouch. That hurts."

"I know it hurts. But it's true. You've been making me feel 'not normal' all summer. I mean. Do you even believe in me?"

"I do! I'm really sorry I hurt you. I believe in you. I do."

We sit in another silence. Now I am the one gulping for air. Eve watches me spin. Then she pats the space beside her. I crawl over and sit in the crook of her arm. She lets me lean hard on her until my breathing is even and slow again.

"Look." She says after a beat. "If I'm being honest sometimes I get jealous. Of you. You know. You never have to worry about getting what Mama has. I do. You're kinda free from that drama . . . like when we go out in public. People don't assume you're just like her. Or that you're with her. That you're . . . sick too."

Free. That's another word I go back to again and again.

(Adjective)—Not bound by the power of another. Able to be and do as one wishes.

"Well I think you're free." I find my voice again. "At least people look at you and can tell you belong. I could get sick too. I have someone's genes too! And we BOTH deal with Mama's moods in public. Or in private. It's hard for me too."

"I know . . ."

"You don't know. You don't know. You don't know." I start

to breathe heavy again. "You act like I'm just like you. But then when you're angry you make me feel like an outsider. That's not fair. It's not my fault you're scared. I am scared all the time."

"Ok. Ok." Eve tries to calm me. But I can feel her heart beating fast too. "I didn't realize I was doing that . . . I'll do better. I promise."

We lean into each other. We inhale and exhale. The blanket gets hot and sweaty. But we don't move. We sit in our hard truths. We float through space. We yell all our fears into the dark. All night long. We talk. We doze. The whole time. Leaning leaning into one another. Like two trees who inherited the same earth. But look up and see very different skies.

Reset

The next morning we undo ourselves from the nest of Eve's bed and brush our teeth standing side by side in the bathroom.

"Cinnamon maple or apple spice?" Eve asks after she spits and rinses.

"Cinna-mi-a-min please!" I say with my mouth still full of foam.

When I get to the kitchen she hands me a steaming bowl of oatmeal and a spoon. "Thanks!" I say.

"No problem." Eve says back.

We join Mama and Papa at the kitchen table and begin spooning food into our mouths as if we haven't eaten in days. Over his paper I watch Papa raise his eyebrow at Mama. Mama shakes her head at him as if to say: *Daniel. Don't make a big deal. Don't ruin this.*

So Papa just grins at us and then takes another swig of coffee. Eve kicks my foot under the table and I kick hers back. We giggle. We shovel more oatmeal into our mouths. Mama takes her meds. Papa slurps his coffee. And if I close my eyes. I can feel a rhythm coming back. Faint but steady.

I Have a Secret Wish

Mama is home

But she is not herself

She walks around

Like this is not her house

Like she is a hotel guest

And even though

She wakes up by eight

Tries to stick to a routine

Meds with her breakfast

A walk on the ditch

An errand or talk therapy

Journaling during lunch

A walk with Papa or us

Before dinner

Dinner and meds

Reading in bed by ten

Sleep ten hours

And repeat

She still does not

Play her violin

She reads to me

Like a robot

She smiles

Like she is somewhere else

Keda girl Keda girl

The Georgia Belles sing

Give it time

Give it time

But I miss her energy

The juneberry red in her cheeks

I wish she wasn't sick

I want her

To tell me I'm hers

And laugh like she used to

Before we moved

Before she tried to end it all

Sometimes I wish

We were still at the cabin

Dancing with the rugs pulled back

Dancing like we'd never stop

New Faces

On Monday Papa drops us off at Mr. John's house for group. Eve and I file in with some of the usual faces: Emma Carl Jesse and Melody. As we take off our shoes in the doorway Vienna runs up and gives Eve a huge hug. Amy and Alyse wave at me from the living room where they are already seated in a circle on the floor.

"Hi Keda. How was your summer?"

I spin around. Huck is standing so close that I accidentally hit him with my book bag.

"Oh sorry. I uh. Good. It was good." I start to say but then my head screams: *Good? It was a mess.* "I mean. It could have been better. How was yours?"

"Same." He says. "Kinda sucked."

I smile at him with relief. But before I can ask why. Mr. John calls us to attention in the other room. Huck and I slide into the circle which to my surprise has grown by a few new faces. Including a girl with teal and black twists in her hair. Big black eyes and long lashes. And skin almost the same muddy color as mine.

"Welcome back everyone!" Mr. John claps. "Let's do a quick

round of names and check in since we have some new people joining us this year. Everyone give me ONE word that describes your summer."

Our words are all over the place. Carl's is *awesome*. Emma's is *confusing*. Vienna's is *stressful*. Eve's is *painful*. Amy's is *dirt*. Alyse's is *short*. Jesse's is *soccer*. I say *messy*. Huck says *never-ending*. And Mr. John just says *work*.

And then the three new faces go. But they get a little more time to introduce themselves.

"I'm Liza." A girl with fiery red hair and hazel eyes starts. She's wearing a loose pair of jeans cowgirl boots and a shirt that has a picture of some band called The Runaways on it. "I'm in 8th grade I guess but I read at a college level. I live on a horse farm. And my summer. I guess the word that describes my summer is 'sunburnt.' Like you can put all the sunscreen you want on me but I'm still gonna be red as a plum. But I just can't be inside all the time you know? I have to be riding or doing chores or just reading under a tree. I can't help it if the sun's out to get me . . ."

"And you can all talk to Liza more about her summer during break!" Mr. John cuts in.

"Right. Sorry." Liza giggles. "I talk a lot. One word? Please."

The girl with twists snorts from across the circle. I watch her roll her eyes at Liza. Liza makes a cross-eyed face back. They both smile.

Next is a sour-faced boy named Tagen. "I'm in the 4th grade. I like *Minecraft*. My summer was 'fine'" is all he says.

Finally. The girl with the teal hair takes her turn. "I'm Jojo." She starts. "Well my full name is Jo-han-na but people get that wrong all the time. I'm in the 6th well I guess the 7th grade now. I just moved here from Ohio with my dad. And my summer was. Well I think someone already said it." She says looking right at me. "But it was 'a mess.'"

"Wow. You all had eventful summers. Even if they were not fun it sounds like you all have a lot to catch up on during our lunch break. Now let's get to business." Mr. John doesn't waste another minute. "It's time to learn how to debate!"

The group groans. Even Huck seems annoyed. But all I can think about is Huck standing so close. And the new girl. And that maybe this homeschool year won't be so bad after all.

Lists

That night. After group. I grab my songbook and write:

THINGS I HAVE IN COMMON WITH JOJO

1. Our melanin is poppin! Obvi. (Jojo is technically mixed. Black dad. White mom.)
2. Both our nicknames have four letters in them.
3. Both of us moved to Albuquerque this year.
4. We both love to sing. (Jojo is going to audition for the New Mexico Youth Choir next month. She's trying to get me to as well.)
5. We have complicated families. (Her parents are divorced. Her mom still lives in Ohio.)
6. We like to read.
7. Neither of us have a cell phone yet but

we made our parents exchange numbers so we can meet at the library soon.

8. Both of us need phones. ASAP. Like yesterday.

Then I turn to the next page and write:

THINGS TO ASK HUCK NEXT GROUP (IF YOU DARE!)

1. Why was your summer "never-ending"?
2. What's your favorite Billie Holiday song?
3. What's your favorite country?
4. Do you want to hang out sometime?
5. Do you like me?

Then I close my songbook and slip it under the rug in my room.

Telling

Two days later I meet Jojo at the library. Mama drops me off and Jojo's dad sets up his laptop in the main room to get some work done.

"My dad's a graphic designer." Jojo says as we head to the youth room. "He 'works from home' a lot. But that's why we moved here so he could work and also homeschool me during the day. He says this job is more flexible than his last one."

"Oh. Cool. I guess my mom kinda 'works from home' too." I say.

We find an empty table in the youth room and sit under it. We'll look for books later. Right now we just pick up where we left off Monday at lunch.

"Favorite color?" Jojo asks.

"Purple."

"Mine's gold or teal. Or gold and teal together."

"I figured." I say pointing to her hair. She's pulled her twists up into a big bun on the top of her head. "I love your hair. Wish I could do that to mine."

"Thanks!" She says. "You can. I mean I got it done in Ohio.

But you know. Your hair's long enough. You could totally get purple twists added in."

"Yeah." I say. Touching my Afro and thinking of the soft leather of Stormy's chair. "Maybe I will. I know a good place to get our hair done. Maybe we can go together sometime?"

"Sure!" Jojo smiles. "I'd like that."

We whisper and laugh. And whisper some more. The youth room is mostly empty since it's the middle of the school day. It's not the willow that Lena and I liked to sit under in Baltimore but it's another kind of hideout.

"So." Jojo starts. "Why was your summer a mess or messy? I mean. If you feel like sharing."

I do. Want to share. But instead I get goose bumps on my arms. I scoot so that I am sitting on top of my hands. I feel them numbing under the weight of my body. I want to tell Jojo everything. To trust that she's not going to turn on me. But after El Rio. After Alma. After my own sister hurting me I am not sure it's a good idea. To share. *We hardly know each other after all.*

But Jojo keeps talking. "Well. I don't mind telling you about my messy summer. I mean. I can tell you won't blab. You know. I think I probably have a bigger mouth than you. But I can keep a secret."

"I can too."

"Well." Jojo says leaning in closer to me. "Another reason we moved here is to get away from my mom. She's an addict. Well I mean it's an illness. Being addicted to pills. And alcohol. And you know. She was doing better. And I really thought they might get together again. But then I guess she started hiding it from my dad. And so here we are. I only saw her every other weekend in Ohio anyway. But still."

Jojo stops talking then. Like she's run out of breath. She hangs her head and picks at a piece of the carpet with her fingers. I can tell she's been holding everything in all summer as well. *Let yourself show.*

"My mom's sick too." I say quietly. And then I let the whole messy story spill out of me.

Imagining Lady Day's Return

I'm reading a book about Billie Holiday. A biography. Mama says it can count toward my history studies. It's so good that I can't put it down. I sit in the sunroom on Sunday flipping the pages as fast as I can.

All this time I knew Billie was singing the blues. But I didn't really understand what she had to be blue about. But Billie had a hard life. When she was just a newborn her dad left her mom. Her mom who was only nineteen (the same age as my birth mother) had to leave Billie with family members all the time while she worked on trains to earn money.

I read about Billie and think about that word *orphan*:

Noun—A child deprived by the death of one or both parents
One who is deprived of parental protection or privilege

About how Billie's parents were both alive but absent. How maybe they tried to protect her but couldn't. How she had to raise herself. How Billie skipped school. Didn't really fit in. How she got sent to juvenile detention. How she worked for years on the streets. How all that lonely. Made her need to sing. How she found the stage and got famous. But how she still hurt and did drugs to numb the hurt. And how her addiction. Her illness. Would one day end her.

I read the whole book in one sitting. I take her story and put it next to mine. Next to Mama's. And I think about Mama playing her violin at Carnegie Hall. On the same stage that Billie sang on in 1948. Just two days after coming out of jail. I think about what music does for women. For me.

I shut my eyes and just imagine I am there. As Billie plants herself center stage that night. As she stands tree still. Her head still stinging where she pricked it. Backstage. Pinning her gardenias in place. How even the photographers standing front and center in the audience must have aimed their enormous steel faces at her. Target practice. Flash! Bull's-eye.

Brava! I can hear a man's voice cry before Billie has even begun. I see her closing her eyes. Purple veins bloom on her thrown-back throat. And then from somewhere her voice escapes. Her gloved arms rise like two ghosts off the sides of her sequined torso. She sings for more than two hours. Thirty-two songs lit in her throat. And then the finale: *Blood on the leaves and blood at the root*. Billie. Lady Day. She burns the house down.

Chances

A couple Mondays later homeschool group meets at our house. During lunch break I sneak away to my room. I grab my songbook and flip to my list. *IF YOU DARE! But do I?* Huck said hello to me again today. And sat close to me in the circle. But I always get sweaty and tongue-tied when I try to say more than three words to him. "What is your problem Keda?" I say to my reflection. "Get it together." But I start to feel dizzy. So I grab a pen and rip a page from my songbook. *Plan B.*

Dear Huck

I wanted to write you an email while you were at Model UN camp. But I was too shy to ask for your address. I feel like we have a lot in common. For example you knew Billie Holiday was a woman. And not many kids our age get that. Anyway. Do you want to hang out sometime? Maybe you can tell me about your favorite Billie song? Or not. We can talk about whatever else too.

Keda

I read it over. I'm running out of time. I'm sure Lena could help me say it better but I have to work quickly. I fold up the note into a tiny square. Then I rush back down the hall toward the sunroom. By the front door is a pile of shoes and bags. I scan the pile for Huck's blue backpack. And then I drop the note into its front pocket before I lose my nerve.

State Capitol

Two Thursdays after I leave Huck the note homeschool group meets at the state capitol building in Santa Fe for a field trip. The building is round instead of square. It is the only round capitol building in the whole United States. We gather on the front steps as everyone arrives. Some parents join us for the day. Others drop off and head into Old Town to have an adventure of their own.

The New Mexico state flag waves high above the building. It is bright yellow with a circular red sun symbol in the middle of it that has lines pointing out in four directions. Mr. John blows the hair back from his forehead and starts a head count. "Ok. Looks like we're just missing Carl and Emma. We'll give them a few more minutes."

I'm standing with Jojo. But she is in a deep conversation with Liza about horses. "I just don't like animals that are bigger than me." Jojo says. But Liza is not having it.

"Oh no. They are very gentle loving animals." Liza protests. "You just have to show them who is boss. You should come to my place sometime. I'll show you. You too Keda. Do you like horses?" She leans over and pats my hand.

"Huh. Yeah. I mean I have never ridden one. But I'd try."

"Ugh. Fine." Jojo says. "If Keda goes. I'll go. But you gotta show us everything Liza."

Liza claps her hands with delight and launches off into planning our visit. I tune out her voice and glance over at Huck. He's reading a plaque by the front entrance. Besides saying a quick hello when we arrived. He's barely acknowledged me. *Go over there.* I will my feet to move but before I can take a step Emma and Carl jump out of a car. And we all head inside for the tour.

Our tour guide tells us the history of New Mexico and the state building. We learn all about the state symbol and flag and we even get to see the room where our senators and representatives debate and vote and pass important laws and policies. Mr. John keeps his comments to a minimum and it is nice to be learning from someone else instead.

After our tour we sit outside in the sun and eat our lunches. Mr. John makes us write a list of questions and reflections. Then he facilitates a short discussion about what we saw. Midway through the discussion I have to pee. I get up and throw my lunch away. I head inside to use the bathroom. When I step back out Huck is there. Filling his water bottle up at the fountains. But when I look. I can see his water bottle is already full. Water overflows onto his hands.

"Hey." I say.

Huck jumps a little. "Hey. I was um. Just getting some more water."

"Oh." I feel my ears get hot. *He wasn't waiting for me.* "Well stay hydrated." I hear myself say as I turn around to go back outside. *Why. Why did I say that?*

"Wait. Keda." Huck is right behind me again. Close. "I uh. Well here." Huck shoves a note into my hands and then practically runs out of the building ahead of me.

I unwrap the note. My toes tingle.

Dear Keda

My favorite Billie Holiday song is "Easy Living." And yes. I'd like to hang out sometime. I'm shy too. Sorry I took so long to write back.

Huck

890-555-6107

And my legs tingle. And my face. And I tuck Huck's note into my pocket. And keep it there. For the rest of the day.

QUESTIONS I HAVE FOR BLACK GIRLS LIKE ME

posted October 17th

Dear L

Are you mad at me? I am worried. You never wrote me after gymnastics camp. Where are you? I've called your mom's cell a bunch of times. Did she tell you I called? Do you hate me? I hope not. I hope you answer soon.

Here are some things that have happened:

1. My mom tried to kill herself. She's doing better now. But nothing is the same and it was a really scary summer. I'll tell you more over the phone.
2. I'm still homeschooled. There is a new girl in group named Jojo (who I think you'd like) and a girl named Liza who is going to teach me to ride a horse. So that will be an adventure.
3. HUCK LIKES ME! I mean. I think. We are going to hang out alone. As friends for now. But we'll see what happens.
4. This summer I realized that adults have just as

many questions as we do. That they don't have all

the answers. Is this what it feels like to grow up?

Lena. I miss you. Write me soon.

XOXO

K

QUESTIONS I HAVE FOR BLACK GIRLS LIKE ME

posted October 19th

Dear K

I am so glad you posted your letter! When I didn't see any posts from you after I got home from camp in August I was hurt. I guess I thought you had forgotten about me. So. I didn't write. And then I just got it in my head that you didn't need me anymore. I know you called a few times. I'm sorry I never re-sponded. I meant to. My mom kept telling me to call you back. But I just couldn't somehow. Stupid. I know. It's hard to know what's going on when we're so far away from each other. I guess I just got insecure. I had no idea what you were going through.

But KEDA. Your mom. I don't even know what to say. I feel so bad. I am going to call you this weekend ok? I can't imagine what I would do if my mom tried to hurt herself. No wonder you didn't write me. And my selfish butt thought you were ghosting on me.

Horseback riding! I am glad you are making some friends. Even if you are a homeschool nerd now. LOL. And of course

Huck likes you. I knew it. Did you guys kiss yet? Are you in love? JKJK. But for real Keda. Kiss him.

Here are some things that happened to me over the summer:

1. I won the gold medal at my regional meet. I know. I know. Go me. ☺
2. My parents got me a cell phone! They surprised me the first day of camp. I mean. It was mostly because they wanted to keep tabs on me. I wasn't even allowed to keep it in my cabin. Camp rules. I had to check it out from the main office when I wanted to call them. I honestly didn't use it that much. I was too busy. But still. I am so excited. Now that I'm home my parents let me keep it on me. I'll email you my number so you can call or computer-text me directly. Ok?
3. I dated this boy at gym camp. Actually. We're still dating. He lives in DC. But we talk all the time. His name is Raphael. OMG. Isn't that so cute? Like the Ninja Turtle. Or maybe it's the painter? Whatever. I'm hoping to visit him soon. If I can convince my mom and dad to take me.

4. And yeah. Adults have no idea what they are doing. They just pretend to.

I hope you know I'm still your #ashyforlife best friend. Even when I'm being insecure.

Your BFF

L

Kin (noun)

Is one of my favorite words. I look it up again after reading Lena's post. I like the way it sounds on my tongue. *Kin.*

A people who come from a common ancestry

One's blood or chosen relatives

Then I start a new post and type a song I've been working on:

posted October 21st

You are my kin

My kind

My kin inside and out

A sister-friend

Full of wonder

And light

With you I am

Always singing

Let's stand side by side

In the sun

Let's be seeds

Smooth and black

Forever growing tall

Stuck in the middle of it all

My kin

My kind

My kin

Inside and out

Family Fridays

In early November Mama Papa Eve and I go roller-skating in the middle of the day. Ever since Mama came home Papa has made an effort to spend Fridays with us. Before his concerts in the evening. So far we've been to the movies. To the zoo. Out to lunch at Sweet Tomato followed by shopping at the mall. And now this week: Roller Palace!

Back in Baltimore Eve and I took ice-skating lessons for about a month. So after a few times around the Roller Palace rink we are coasting. Papa and Mama not so much. They stay at the very edges of the rink and take baby steps but still somehow end up falling on their butts every five minutes.

"Help us!" Mama screams with laughter as she tries to untangle Papa's legs from hers. I zoom up and stop in front of them. I try pulling Mama up but she flails and falls again. Papa rolls onto the rug next to the rink and then stands up by getting on his knees first and crawling for a bit like a baby.

"Well. I guess you two should stick to playing music then." Eve has zoomed up behind me. She is smiling as well. "You guys suck at this."

And as she says that Mama rolls off the rink onto the rug. And crawls like a baby toward the benches. She is laughing so hard that her whole body shakes.

"That's it!" She says. "I'm calling it. I give up."

Papa who has managed to stand baby scoots over to her. He is red in the face. His smile crooked and loose. "Me too!"

"Girls!" Mama says then. "Show us what you got. I think we're gonna stay here and get some food." She unlaces her skates and then helps Papa with his.

Eve and I zip and dip and twirl and zoom. And it is almost like flying. When the lights come up for an "under 8 only skate" we look for Mama and Papa in the food court but they are nowhere to be found. My hands get sweaty.

"Did they leave us?" I choke.

"No. They wouldn't do that. There they are." Eve points toward the arcade. Mama and Papa are in their socked feet. Playing a heated game of air hockey. Every time Papa makes a goal Mama screams: "DANIEL NOT SO HARD!" and then breaks into a fit of laughter.

And Papa is giggling as well. Making faces at her. And joking about how slow she is. Even though he too flinches every time Mama slams the puck back to his side.

"And that" Eve jokes motioning toward our parents "is why we don't play sports in this family."

"For real." I say.

But instead of going back to the rink. The two of us join in. Mama and me against Papa and Eve. And we play so many games before we know it it's closing time and we're getting kicked out. And we're laughing so hard we don't even care.

Mama Is in the Earth

I am dreaming. I walk hand in hand with my sister through a silver field. The Georgia Belles follow behind us. Humming. Humming. Guiding us on. Eve throws her head back and howls like a wild dog. I do the same. Our howling pulls in the day. The sunrise sprinting over the land. Mama and Papa are nowhere to be found. Eve and I run and run and run. Our legs pumping. Then we collapse and the world spins.

Mama's violin is in the earth. No. Mama is in the earth. We giggle and press our ears to the ground. We hear Mama playing her strings hard and fast. We dig a hole and climb into the earth. The earth looks like the inside of a piano. Mama is in the center. Between two ribs of the soundboard. She is furious with movement. Her eyes are closed and she doesn't see us. We sit and watch her play. She plays all night long.

And when I wake up the next morning she is still playing. But I am in my own bed. I throw off my sheets and put on my robe. It's early. Maybe 6am? I creep down the hallway. Mama is in the living room. By the piano. She's wearing her nightgown and her hair is undone. But she's playing! A slow painful song that gets faster and faster as the sun rises. I sit at the edge of the hallway and listen. She is glowing. Her red cheeks flushed. She sways and dips and moves her arm like a delicate saw over the strings. I close my eyes. I never want her to stop.

Lessons

Eventually Mama stops playing. "You can come closer little bird." Mama calls to me. "I don't mind."

I scurry to sit on the rug in front of her.

"It's been too long." She says then. "I forgot how good it feels."

"I thought I was dreaming when I heard you. What song is that?"

"I don't know. I made it up."

"That's what I like to do. Make up songs. It helps me. Feel better. Well sometimes."

Mama smiles and then looks at me long. "I'm so sorry. I know I put you and your sister through a lot over the summer but I'm trying now Makeda. And it makes me so proud to see the ways you are growing up. Into a strong young woman."

I don't say anything and Mama starts another song. This time she puts down her bow and plucks and picks at her strings with her pointer finger. When she stops playing I let the question I have been holding holding holding on to escape.

"Mama." I start. "Are you going to try to. You know. Hurt yourself again?"

She wraps her violin in scarves and puts it in its case before sitting down next to me on the rug. "I love you Makeda. You know that? At least I hope you do."

"But . . . are you going to leave me. Leave us?" I ask again.

I can feel Mama tensing next to me. She and I sit next to each other but we look at the piano in front of us. Mama grabs my hand. Hers is shaking.

"Here's what I love about you." She continues. "You see all the smallest details about the world. It's a little scary how much you see. But you are curious and observant and even when you see hard things you don't turn away."

But do you want to live? My head echoes.

"Look. With my illness I can't really promise anything. And I have to spend some time figuring out how to live with this. How to love myself. How to get back to my music even when the meds make me fuzzy. If I have another manic episode I might have to go away again. But no matter what I do. Or where I go. Or what my mood is. You have to know I love you and your sister."

"Ok." I say. But it feels like I have stones in my throat. I am heavy with knowing. *A mother hurts. You cannot stop the hurt.*

"Listen." Mama says then grabbing my chin and turning my head to look her in the eyes. "I was thinking. Maybe we should get you some singing lessons huh?"

"Instead of piano!" I almost shout.

Mama laughs. "No. No. Piano is still mandatory. This would be in addition. I think maybe it's time to get you some formal training. Would you like that?"

I shake my head yes and smile.

Mama kisses me on the chin. "Good." She says. "Good."

Flung

That night. The night after I find Mama and her violin in the earth. I do not get up once to check the locks. The door. To listen to my mama my sister my papa breathing.

Instead. When the house gets quiet. I burrow down deep into my covers. I sleep. I do not fidget or fight or tangle with my sheets. I do not twist and turn.

At dawn the late-November sun begins to filter through my blinds. And I wake up to a soft rattling in my bones. Drums in my rib cage. Voices in my ears. But no swaying bodies. No shadows in my room. Just light.

Where are you? I say. Knowing the answer already. But for just a moment wanting them back.

Baby girl

We are inside inside

Bum-bum-bum

Do-wee-do-wee

Feel our love

And make it yours

Inside inside bum-bum-bum

Where we're all strong

Dee-dee-leedl-wee

Keda girl Keda girl

What do you know?

Sing it sing it sing it so

Fling yourself

From that tree

Peachy girl

You are ripe

You are

Your own magic

You don't need us to be free

All you need is a song

Diddlee-do-eee

So I fling my blinds open. I open my mouth. I smear my ripe voice all over the morning. And let it ring.

What I Know

I am a girl becoming a woman. People throw their puzzled looks at me and I know they're wondering: *Who does she look like?* But I am learning to say: *Me. I look like me.* I am a girl becoming a woman. My skin is a home and a hurt. I look in the mirror and see a mother I've never met. My mama looks at me with love but doesn't always see my struggle. I have kin in places I never even knew. I am strong even when I feel scared. I open my mouth and songs spill out. *I love. I hurt. I wonder. I love. I hurt. I wonder.* That's the blues. And I sing it loud. I sing it true. You can't stop the blues. You just have to trust your heart and let them pour out of you.

Acknowledgments

First and foremost, all my love and gratitude to my parents! Thank you for instilling a deep appreciation of music and art within me from a young age, and for providing me with countless opportunities to harness my creativity. And to my beautiful siblings—you inspire and motivate me every day to be better and love harder. I love you all.

It truly takes a village to raise a book, and I feel so grateful for the mentorship of Camille T. Dungy and Tayari Jones. Thank you both for guiding me in and out of the classroom, supporting my work, and setting such shining examples of what it looks like to be a writer in this world.

Immense gratitude to my agent, Jane Dystel, who took a chance on me and has been a champion for my work. Thank you to my wonderful editor, Joy Peskin, who has been instrumental in uplifting my vision and story. I am honored to have shared this journey with you.

Thank you, Tomi Obaro, Saeed Jones, and *Buzzfeed News Reader*, for giving me a platform to share my own adoptee story which in turn inspired Makeda's story.

All my gratitude to the following institutions and writing organizations that helped shape and guide me: Interlochen Arts Academy, the University of Michigan Residential College, San Francisco State University, the Neutral Zone, 826 National, Cave Canem, Voices of Our Nations Arts Foundation, and Breadloaf Writers' Conference. And thank you to the many teachers and mentors who supported me along the way: Jack Driscoll, Michael Delp, Jeff Kass, Gerald Richards, Jen Benka, Ken Mikolowski, Megan Sweeney, Toni Mirosevich, and r. erica doyle.

Thank you to the following journals and presses for publishing drafts of some of the pieces in this book: *Prelude* magazine, *Bodega* magazine, and Damaged Goods Press.

I would be nothing without the support of my fierce writer community and chosen family: Liz Latty, Yalie Kamara, Molly Raynor, Lauren Whitehead, and José Vadi. The group works! Thank you for reading my messy drafts, giving me pep talks, and believing in me. You are my hearts. Nate and Reed—you know I love you, too! Thanks for being the #team for life.

Much love and gratitude to Chris Jennings and Dan Lau, for braving that MFA life and providing me with support, friendship, and necessary dance parties.

A big shout-out to the 2017 Heart & Sole Team at MacDonald Middle School: your bright voices and self-determination taught me so much as I was writing this book!

Taia Brymer: I am so appreciative that you and I were able to share our stories and experiences with one another. Makeda's story is stronger because of you.

Laura and Kenny Raynor: Thank you for always making a place for me and my family at your table. For reading my work and cheering me on. I am so lucky to have you in my life.

Thank you, Shani! Because of you I learned to heal and live more honestly while writing this book. For this I am deeply grateful.

All my love to Ray and CV for cheering me on, and for making me smile and feel loved every day.

To my beloved childhood friends: Jessye, Leah, and Lil Lizzie. Thank you for being my kin.

Finally, I am grateful to my partner, Vanessa. Whose love, support, feedback, and motivation helped push me forward with this project on so many different occasions. And also to my little dog, Henry. For warming my feet and keeping me and my characters company on so many long writing days. I love you both.